I0541052

A Midsummer Night's Dream

&

The Sonnets

William Shakespeare

A Midsummer Night's Dream & The Sonnets

Copyright © 2021 Bibliotech Press
All rights reserved

The present edition is a reproduction of previous publication of this classic work. Minor typographical errors may have been corrected without note; however, for an authentic reading experience the spelling, punctuation, and capitalization have been retained from the original text.

ISBN: 978-1-63637-598-4

CONTENTS

A MIDSUMMER NIGHT'S DREAM

A MIDSUMMER NIGHT'S DREAM

DRAMATIS PERSONÆ

THESEUS, Duke of Athens
HIPPOLYTA, Queen of the Amazons, bethrothed to Theseus
EGEUS, Father to Hermia
HERMIA, daughter to Egeus, in love with Lysander
HELENA, in love with Demetrius
LYSANDER, in love with Hermia
DEMETRIUS, in love with Hermia
PHILOSTRATE, Master of the Revels to Theseus
QUINCE, the Carpenter
SNUG, the Joiner
BOTTOM, the Weaver
FLUTE, the Bellows-mender
SNOUT, the Tinker
STARVELING, the Tailor
OBERON, King of the Fairies
TITANIA, Queen of the Fairies
PUCK, or ROBIN GOODFELLOW, a Fairy
PEASEBLOSSOM, Fairy
COBWEB, Fairy
MOTH, Fairy
MUSTARDSEED, Fairy
PYRAMUS, THISBE, WALL, MOONSHINE, LION; Characters in
the Interlude performed by the Clowns

Other Fairies attending their King and Queen
Attendants on Theseus and Hippolyta

ACT I

SCENE I

Athens. A room in the Palace of Theseus

Enter Theseus, Hippolyta, Philostrate and Attendants.

THESEUS.
Now, fair Hippolyta, our nuptial hour
Draws on apace; four happy days bring in
Another moon; but oh, methinks, how slow
This old moon wanes! She lingers my desires,
Like to a step-dame or a dowager,
Long withering out a young man's revenue.

HIPPOLYTA.
Four days will quickly steep themselves in night;
Four nights will quickly dream away the time;
And then the moon, like to a silver bow
New bent in heaven, shall behold the night
Of our solemnities.

THESEUS.
Go, Philostrate,
Stir up the Athenian youth to merriments;
Awake the pert and nimble spirit of mirth;
Turn melancholy forth to funerals;
The pale companion is not for our pomp.

[*Exit Philostrate.*]

Hippolyta, I woo'd thee with my sword,
And won thy love doing thee injuries;

2

But I will wed thee in another key,
With pomp, with triumph, and with revelling.

Enter Egeus, Hermia, Lysander and Demetrius.

EGEUS.
Happy be Theseus, our renownèd Duke!

THESEUS.
Thanks, good Egeus. What's the news with thee?

EGEUS.
Full of vexation come I, with complaint
Against my child, my daughter Hermia.
Stand forth, Demetrius. My noble lord,
This man hath my consent to marry her.
Stand forth, Lysander. And, my gracious Duke,
This man hath bewitch'd the bosom of my child.
Thou, thou, Lysander, thou hast given her rhymes,
And interchang'd love-tokens with my child.
Thou hast by moonlight at her window sung,
With feigning voice, verses of feigning love;
And stol'n the impression of her fantasy
With bracelets of thy hair, rings, gauds, conceits,
Knacks, trifles, nosegays, sweetmeats (messengers
Of strong prevailment in unharden'd youth)
With cunning hast thou filch'd my daughter's heart,
Turn'd her obedience (which is due to me)
To stubborn harshness. And, my gracious Duke,
Be it so she will not here before your grace
Consent to marry with Demetrius,
I beg the ancient privilege of Athens:
As she is mine I may dispose of her;
Which shall be either to this gentleman
Or to her death, according to our law
Immediately provided in that case.

THESEUS.
What say you, Hermia? Be advis'd, fair maid.
To you your father should be as a god;
One that compos'd your beauties, yea, and one
To whom you are but as a form in wax
By him imprinted, and within his power
To leave the figure, or disfigure it.
Demetrius is a worthy gentleman.

3

HERMIA.
So is Lysander.

THESEUS.
In himself he is.
But in this kind, wanting your father's voice,
The other must be held the worthier.

HERMIA.
I would my father look'd but with my eyes.

THESEUS.
Rather your eyes must with his judgment look.

HERMIA.
I do entreat your Grace to pardon me.
I know not by what power I am made bold,
Nor how it may concern my modesty
In such a presence here to plead my thoughts:
But I beseech your Grace that I may know
The worst that may befall me in this case,
If I refuse to wed Demetrius.

THESEUS.
Either to die the death, or to abjure
For ever the society of men.
Therefore, fair Hermia, question your desires,
Know of your youth, examine well your blood,
Whether, if you yield not to your father's choice,
You can endure the livery of a nun,
For aye to be in shady cloister mew'd,
To live a barren sister all your life,
Chanting faint hymns to the cold fruitless moon.
Thrice-blessèd they that master so their blood
To undergo such maiden pilgrimage,
But earthlier happy is the rose distill'd
Than that which, withering on the virgin thorn,
Grows, lives, and dies, in single blessedness.

HERMIA.
So will I grow, so live, so die, my lord,
Ere I will yield my virgin patent up
Unto his lordship, whose unwishèd yoke
My soul consents not to give sovereignty.

THESEUS.
Take time to pause; and by the next new moon
The sealing-day betwixt my love and me
For everlasting bond of fellowship,
Upon that day either prepare to die
For disobedience to your father's will,
Or else to wed Demetrius, as he would,
Or on Diana's altar to protest
For aye austerity and single life.

DEMETRIUS.
Relent, sweet Hermia; and, Lysander, yield
Thy crazèd title to my certain right.

LYSANDER.
You have her father's love, Demetrius.
Let me have Hermia's. Do you marry him.

EGEUS.
Scornful Lysander, true, he hath my love;
And what is mine my love shall render him;
And she is mine, and all my right of her
I do estate unto Demetrius.

LYSANDER.
I am, my lord, as well deriv'd as he,
As well possess'd; my love is more than his;
My fortunes every way as fairly rank'd,
If not with vantage, as Demetrius';
And, which is more than all these boasts can be,
I am belov'd of beauteous Hermia.
Why should not I then prosecute my right?
Demetrius, I'll avouch it to his head,
Made love to Nedar's daughter, Helena,
And won her soul; and she, sweet lady, dotes,
Devoutly dotes, dotes in idolatry,
Upon this spotted and inconstant man.

THESEUS.
I must confess that I have heard so much,
And with Demetrius thought to have spoke thereof;
But, being over-full of self-affairs,
My mind did lose it.—But, Demetrius, come,
And come, Egeus; you shall go with me.
I have some private schooling for you both.—

For you, fair Hermia, look you arm yourself
To fit your fancies to your father's will,
Or else the law of Athens yields you up
(Which by no means we may extenuate)
To death, or to a vow of single life.
Come, my Hippolyta. What cheer, my love?
Demetrius and Egeus, go along;
I must employ you in some business
Against our nuptial, and confer with you
Of something nearly that concerns yourselves.

EGEUS.
With duty and desire we follow you.

[*Exeunt all but Lysander and Hermia.*]

LYSANDER.
How now, my love? Why is your cheek so pale?
How chance the roses there do fade so fast?

HERMIA.
Belike for want of rain, which I could well
Beteem them from the tempest of my eyes.

LYSANDER.
Ay me! For aught that I could ever read,
Could ever hear by tale or history,
The course of true love never did run smooth.
But either it was different in blood—

HERMIA.
O cross! Too high to be enthrall'd to low.

LYSANDER.
Or else misgraffèd in respect of years—

HERMIA.
O spite! Too old to be engag'd to young.

LYSANDER.
Or else it stood upon the choice of friends—

HERMIA.
O hell! to choose love by another's eyes!

LYSANDER.
Or, if there were a sympathy in choice,
War, death, or sickness did lay siege to it,
Making it momentany as a sound,
Swift as a shadow, short as any dream,
Brief as the lightning in the collied night
That, in a spleen, unfolds both heaven and earth,
And, ere a man hath power to say, 'Behold!'
The jaws of darkness do devour it up:
So quick bright things come to confusion.

HERMIA.
If then true lovers have ever cross'd,
It stands as an edict in destiny.
Then let us teach our trial patience,
Because it is a customary cross,
As due to love as thoughts and dreams and sighs,
Wishes and tears, poor fancy's followers.

LYSANDER.
A good persuasion; therefore, hear me, Hermia.
I have a widow aunt, a dowager
Of great revenue, and she hath no child.
From Athens is her house remote seven leagues,
And she respects me as her only son.
There, gentle Hermia, may I marry thee,
And to that place the sharp Athenian law
Cannot pursue us. If thou lovest me then,
Steal forth thy father's house tomorrow night;
And in the wood, a league without the town
(Where I did meet thee once with Helena
To do observance to a morn of May),
There will I stay for thee.

HERMIA.
My good Lysander!
I swear to thee by Cupid's strongest bow,
By his best arrow with the golden head,
By the simplicity of Venus' doves,
By that which knitteth souls and prospers loves,
And by that fire which burn'd the Carthage queen
When the false Trojan under sail was seen,
By all the vows that ever men have broke
(In number more than ever women spoke),

In that same place thou hast appointed me,
Tomorrow truly will I meet with thee.

LYSANDER.
Keep promise, love. Look, here comes Helena.

Enter Helena.

HERMIA.
God speed fair Helena! Whither away?

HELENA.
Call you me fair? That fair again unsay.
Demetrius loves your fair. O happy fair!
Your eyes are lode-stars and your tongue's sweet air
More tuneable than lark to shepherd's ear,
When wheat is green, when hawthorn buds appear.
Sickness is catching. O were favour so,
Yours would I catch, fair Hermia, ere I go.
My ear should catch your voice, my eye your eye,
My tongue should catch your tongue's sweet melody.
Were the world mine, Demetrius being bated,
The rest I'd give to be to you translated.
O, teach me how you look, and with what art
You sway the motion of Demetrius' heart!

HERMIA.
I frown upon him, yet he loves me still.

HELENA.
O that your frowns would teach my smiles such skill!

HERMIA.
I give him curses, yet he gives me love.

HELENA.
O that my prayers could such affection move!

HERMIA.
The more I hate, the more he follows me.

HELENA.
The more I love, the more he hateth me.

HERMIA.
His folly, Helena, is no fault of mine.

HELENA.
None but your beauty; would that fault were mine!

HERMIA.
Take comfort: he no more shall see my face;
Lysander and myself will fly this place.
Before the time I did Lysander see,
Seem'd Athens as a paradise to me.
O, then, what graces in my love do dwell,
That he hath turn'd a heaven into hell!

LYSANDER.
Helen, to you our minds we will unfold:
Tomorrow night, when Phoebe doth behold
Her silver visage in the watery glass,
Decking with liquid pearl the bladed grass
(A time that lovers' flights doth still conceal),
Through Athens' gates have we devis'd to steal.

HERMIA.
And in the wood where often you and I
Upon faint primrose beds were wont to lie,
Emptying our bosoms of their counsel sweet,
There my Lysander and myself shall meet,
And thence from Athens turn away our eyes,
To seek new friends and stranger companies.
Farewell, sweet playfellow. Pray thou for us,
And good luck grant thee thy Demetrius!
Keep word, Lysander. We must starve our sight
From lovers' food, till morrow deep midnight.

LYSANDER.
I will, my Hermia.

[*Exit Hermia.*]

Helena, adieu.
As you on him, Demetrius dote on you!

[*Exit Lysander.*]

HELENA.
How happy some o'er other some can be!
Through Athens I am thought as fair as she.
But what of that? Demetrius thinks not so;

He will not know what all but he do know.
And as he errs, doting on Hermia's eyes,
So I, admiring of his qualities.
Things base and vile, holding no quantity,
Love can transpose to form and dignity.
Love looks not with the eyes, but with the mind;
And therefore is wing'd Cupid painted blind.
Nor hath love's mind of any judgment taste.
Wings, and no eyes, figure unheedy haste.
And therefore is love said to be a child,
Because in choice he is so oft beguil'd.
As waggish boys in game themselves forswear,
So the boy Love is perjur'd everywhere.
For, ere Demetrius look'd on Hermia's eyne,
He hail'd down oaths that he was only mine;
And when this hail some heat from Hermia felt,
So he dissolv'd, and showers of oaths did melt.
I will go tell him of fair Hermia's flight.
Then to the wood will he tomorrow night
Pursue her; and for this intelligence
If I have thanks, it is a dear expense.
But herein mean I to enrich my pain,
To have his sight thither and back again.

[*Exit Helena.*]

SCENE II

The Same. A Room in a Cottage

Enter Quince, Snug, Bottom, Flute, Snout and Starveling.

QUINCE.
Is all our company here?

BOTTOM.
You were best to call them generally, man by man, according to the scrip.

QUINCE.
Here is the scroll of every man's name, which is thought fit through all Athens, to play in our interlude before the Duke and Duchess, on his wedding-day at night.

BOTTOM.
First, good Peter Quince, say what the play treats on; then read the names of the actors; and so grow to a point.

QUINCE.
Marry, our play is *The most lamentable comedy and most cruel death of Pyramus and Thisbe.*

BOTTOM.
A very good piece of work, I assure you, and a merry. Now, good Peter Quince, call forth your actors by the scroll. Masters, spread yourselves.

QUINCE.
Answer, as I call you. Nick Bottom, the weaver.

BOTTOM.
Ready. Name what part I am for, and proceed.

QUINCE.
You, Nick Bottom, are set down for Pyramus.

11

BOTTOM.
What is Pyramus—a lover, or a tyrant?

QUINCE.
A lover, that kills himself most gallantly for love.

BOTTOM.
That will ask some tears in the true performing of it. If I do it, let the
audience look to their eyes. I will move storms; I will condole in
some measure. To the rest—yet my chief humour is for a tyrant. I
could play Ercles rarely, or a part to tear a cat in, to make all split.

> The raging rocks
> And shivering shocks
> Shall break the locks
>   Of prison gates,
> And Phibbus' car
> Shall shine from far,
> And make and mar
>   The foolish Fates.

This was lofty. Now name the rest of the players. This is Ercles' vein,
a tyrant's vein; a lover is more condoling.

QUINCE.
Francis Flute, the bellows-mender.

FLUTE.
Here, Peter Quince.

QUINCE.
Flute, you must take Thisbe on you.

FLUTE.
What is Thisbe? A wandering knight?

QUINCE.
It is the lady that Pyramus must love.

FLUTE.
Nay, faith, let not me play a woman. I have a beard coming.

QUINCE.
That's all one. You shall play it in a mask, and you may speak as
small as you will.

BOTTOM.
And I may hide my face, let me play Thisbe too. I'll speak in a monstrous little voice; 'Thisne, Thisne!'—'Ah, Pyramus, my lover dear! thy Thisbe dear! and lady dear!'

QUINCE.
No, no, you must play Pyramus; and, Flute, you Thisbe.

BOTTOM.
Well, proceed.

QUINCE.
Robin Starveling, the tailor.

STARVELING.
Here, Peter Quince.

QUINCE.
Robin Starveling, you must play Thisbe's mother.
Tom Snout, the tinker.

SNOUT
Here, Peter Quince.

QUINCE.
You, Pyramus' father; myself, Thisbe's father;
Snug, the joiner, you, the lion's part. And, I hope here is a play fitted.

SNUG
Have you the lion's part written? Pray you, if it be, give it me, for I am slow of study.

QUINCE.
You may do it extempore, for it is nothing but roaring.

BOTTOM.
Let me play the lion too. I will roar that I will do any man's heart good to hear me. I will roar that I will make the Duke say 'Let him roar again, let him roar again.'

QUINCE.
If you should do it too terribly, you would fright the Duchess and the ladies, that they would shriek; and that were enough to hang us all.

13

ALL
That would hang us every mother's son.

BOTTOM.
I grant you, friends, if you should fright the ladies out of their wits, they would have no more discretion but to hang us. But I will aggravate my voice so, that I will roar you as gently as any sucking dove; I will roar you an 'twere any nightingale.

QUINCE.
You can play no part but Pyramus, for Pyramus is a sweet-faced man; a proper man as one shall see in a summer's day; a most lovely gentleman-like man. Therefore you must needs play Pyramus.

BOTTOM.
Well, I will undertake it. What beard were I best to play it in?

QUINCE.
Why, what you will.

BOTTOM.
I will discharge it in either your straw-colour beard, your orange-tawny beard, your purple-in-grain beard, or your French-crown-colour beard, your perfect yellow.

QUINCE.
Some of your French crowns have no hair at all, and then you will play bare-faced. But, masters, here are your parts, and I am to entreat you, request you, and desire you, to con them by tomorrow night; and meet me in the palace wood, a mile without the town, by moonlight; there will we rehearse, for if we meet in the city, we shall be dogg'd with company, and our devices known. In the meantime I will draw a bill of properties, such as our play wants. I pray you fail me not.

BOTTOM.
We will meet, and there we may rehearse most obscenely and courageously. Take pains, be perfect; adieu.

QUINCE.
At the Duke's oak we meet.

BOTTOM.
Enough. Hold, or cut bow-strings.

[*Exeunt.*]

14

ACT II

SCENE I

A wood near Athens

Enter a Fairy at one door, and Puck at another.

PUCK.
How now, spirit! Whither wander you?

FAIRY
  Over hill, over dale,
    Thorough bush, thorough brier,
  Over park, over pale,
    Thorough flood, thorough fire,
  I do wander everywhere,
  Swifter than the moon's sphere;
  And I serve the Fairy Queen,
  To dew her orbs upon the green.
  The cowslips tall her pensioners be,
  In their gold coats spots you see;
  Those be rubies, fairy favours,
  In those freckles live their savours.
I must go seek some dew-drops here,
And hang a pearl in every cowslip's ear.
Farewell, thou lob of spirits; I'll be gone.
Our Queen and all her elves come here anon.

PUCK.
The King doth keep his revels here tonight;
Take heed the Queen come not within his sight,
For Oberon is passing fell and wrath,
Because that she, as her attendant, hath
A lovely boy, stol'n from an Indian king;

She never had so sweet a changeling.
And jealous Oberon would have the child
Knight of his train, to trace the forests wild:
But she perforce withholds the lovèd boy,
Crowns him with flowers, and makes him all her joy.
And now they never meet in grove or green,
By fountain clear, or spangled starlight sheen,
But they do square; that all their elves for fear
Creep into acorn cups, and hide them there.

FAIRY
Either I mistake your shape and making quite,
Or else you are that shrewd and knavish sprite
Call'd Robin Goodfellow. Are not you he
That frights the maidens of the villagery,
Skim milk, and sometimes labour in the quern,
And bootless make the breathless housewife churn,
And sometime make the drink to bear no barm,
Mislead night-wanderers, laughing at their harm?
Those that Hobgoblin call you, and sweet Puck,
You do their work, and they shall have good luck.
Are not you he?

PUCK.
Thou speak'st aright;
I am that merry wanderer of the night.
I jest to Oberon, and make him smile,
When I a fat and bean-fed horse beguile,
Neighing in likeness of a filly foal;
And sometime lurk I in a gossip's bowl
In very likeness of a roasted crab,
And, when she drinks, against her lips I bob,
And on her withered dewlap pour the ale.
The wisest aunt, telling the saddest tale,
Sometime for three-foot stool mistaketh me;
Then slip I from her bum, down topples she,
And 'tailor' cries, and falls into a cough;
And then the whole quire hold their hips and loffe
And waxen in their mirth, and neeze, and swear
A merrier hour was never wasted there.
But room, fairy. Here comes Oberon.

FAIRY
And here my mistress. Would that he were gone!

Enter Oberon at one door, with his Train, and Titania at another,
with hers.

OBERON.
Ill met by moonlight, proud Titania.

TITANIA.
What, jealous Oberon! Fairies, skip hence;
I have forsworn his bed and company.

OBERON.
Tarry, rash wanton; am not I thy lord?

TITANIA.
Then I must be thy lady; but I know
When thou hast stol'n away from fairyland,
And in the shape of Corin sat all day
Playing on pipes of corn, and versing love
To amorous Phillida. Why art thou here,
Come from the farthest steep of India,
But that, forsooth, the bouncing Amazon,
Your buskin'd mistress and your warrior love,
To Theseus must be wedded; and you come
To give their bed joy and prosperity?

OBERON.
How canst thou thus, for shame, Titania,
Glance at my credit with Hippolyta,
Knowing I know thy love to Theseus?
Didst not thou lead him through the glimmering night
From Perigenia, whom he ravished?
And make him with fair Aegles break his faith,
With Ariadne and Antiopa?

TITANIA.
These are the forgeries of jealousy:
And never, since the middle summer's spring,
Met we on hill, in dale, forest, or mead,
By pavèd fountain, or by rushy brook,
Or on the beachèd margent of the sea,
To dance our ringlets to the whistling wind,
But with thy brawls thou hast disturb'd our sport.
Therefore the winds, piping to us in vain,
As in revenge, have suck'd up from the sea
Contagious fogs; which, falling in the land,

Hath every pelting river made so proud
That they have overborne their continents.
The ox hath therefore stretch'd his yoke in vain,
The ploughman lost his sweat, and the green corn
Hath rotted ere his youth attain'd a beard.
The fold stands empty in the drownèd field,
And crows are fatted with the murrion flock;
The nine-men's-morris is fill'd up with mud,
And the quaint mazes in the wanton green,
For lack of tread, are undistinguishable.
The human mortals want their winter here.
No night is now with hymn or carol blest.
Therefore the moon, the governess of floods,
Pale in her anger, washes all the air,
That rheumatic diseases do abound.
And thorough this distemperature we see
The seasons alter: hoary-headed frosts
Fall in the fresh lap of the crimson rose;
And on old Hiems' thin and icy crown
An odorous chaplet of sweet summer buds
Is, as in mockery, set. The spring, the summer,
The childing autumn, angry winter, change
Their wonted liveries; and the mazed world,
By their increase, now knows not which is which.
And this same progeny of evils comes
From our debate, from our dissension;
We are their parents and original.

OBERON.
Do you amend it, then. It lies in you.
Why should Titania cross her Oberon?
I do but beg a little changeling boy
To be my henchman.

TITANIA.
Set your heart at rest;
The fairyland buys not the child of me.
His mother was a vot'ress of my order,
And in the spicèd Indian air, by night,
Full often hath she gossip'd by my side;
And sat with me on Neptune's yellow sands,
Marking th' embarkèd traders on the flood,
When we have laugh'd to see the sails conceive,
And grow big-bellied with the wanton wind;

Which she, with pretty and with swimming gait
Following (her womb then rich with my young squire),
Would imitate, and sail upon the land,
To fetch me trifles, and return again,
As from a voyage, rich with merchandise.
But she, being mortal, of that boy did die;
And for her sake do I rear up her boy,
And for her sake I will not part with him.

OBERON.
How long within this wood intend you stay?

TITANIA.
Perchance till after Theseus' wedding-day.
If you will patiently dance in our round,
And see our moonlight revels, go with us;
If not, shun me, and I will spare your haunts.

OBERON.
Give me that boy and I will go with thee.

TITANIA.
Not for thy fairy kingdom. Fairies, away.
We shall chide downright if I longer stay.

[*Exit Titania with her Train.*]

OBERON.
Well, go thy way. Thou shalt not from this grove
Till I torment thee for this injury.—
My gentle Puck, come hither. Thou rememb'rest
Since once I sat upon a promontory,
And heard a mermaid on a dolphin's back
Uttering such dulcet and harmonious breath
That the rude sea grew civil at her song
And certain stars shot madly from their spheres
To hear the sea-maid's music.

PUCK.
I remember.

OBERON.
That very time I saw, (but thou couldst not),
Flying between the cold moon and the earth,
Cupid all arm'd: a certain aim he took

At a fair vestal, thronèd by the west,
And loos'd his love-shaft smartly from his bow
As it should pierce a hundred thousand hearts.
But I might see young Cupid's fiery shaft
Quench'd in the chaste beams of the watery moon;
And the imperial votress passed on,
In maiden meditation, fancy-free.
Yet mark'd I where the bolt of Cupid fell:
It fell upon a little western flower,
Before milk-white, now purple with love's wound,
And maidens call it love-in-idleness.
Fetch me that flower, the herb I showed thee once:
The juice of it on sleeping eyelids laid
Will make or man or woman madly dote
Upon the next live creature that it sees.
Fetch me this herb, and be thou here again
Ere the leviathan can swim a league.

PUCK.
I'll put a girdle round about the earth
In forty minutes.

[*Exit Puck.*]

OBERON.
Having once this juice,
I'll watch Titania when she is asleep,
And drop the liquor of it in her eyes:
The next thing then she waking looks upon
(Be it on lion, bear, or wolf, or bull,
On meddling monkey, or on busy ape)
She shall pursue it with the soul of love.
And ere I take this charm from off her sight
(As I can take it with another herb)
I'll make her render up her page to me.
But who comes here? I am invisible;
And I will overhear their conference.

Enter Demetrius, Helena *following him.*

DEMETRIUS.
I love thee not, therefore pursue me not.
Where is Lysander and fair Hermia?
The one I'll slay, the other slayeth me.
Thou told'st me they were stol'n into this wood,

And here am I, and wode within this wood
Because I cannot meet with Hermia.
Hence, get thee gone, and follow me no more.

HELENA.
You draw me, you hard-hearted adamant,
But yet you draw not iron, for my heart
Is true as steel. Leave you your power to draw,
And I shall have no power to follow you.

DEMETRIUS.
Do I entice you? Do I speak you fair?
Or rather do I not in plainest truth
Tell you I do not, nor I cannot love you?

HELENA.
And even for that do I love you the more.
I am your spaniel; and, Demetrius,
The more you beat me, I will fawn on you.
Use me but as your spaniel, spurn me, strike me,
Neglect me, lose me; only give me leave,
Unworthy as I am, to follow you.
What worser place can I beg in your love,
(And yet a place of high respect with me)
Than to be usèd as you use your dog?

DEMETRIUS.
Tempt not too much the hatred of my spirit;
For I am sick when I do look on thee.

HELENA.
And I am sick when I look not on you.

DEMETRIUS.
You do impeach your modesty too much
To leave the city and commit yourself
Into the hands of one that loves you not,
To trust the opportunity of night.
And the ill counsel of a desert place,
With the rich worth of your virginity.

HELENA.
Your virtue is my privilege: for that.
It is not night when I do see your face,
Therefore I think I am not in the night;

21

Nor doth this wood lack worlds of company,
For you, in my respect, are all the world.
Then how can it be said I am alone
When all the world is here to look on me?

DEMETRIUS.
I'll run from thee and hide me in the brakes,
And leave thee to the mercy of wild beasts.

HELENA.
The wildest hath not such a heart as you.
Run when you will, the story shall be chang'd;
Apollo flies, and Daphne holds the chase;
The dove pursues the griffin, the mild hind
Makes speed to catch the tiger. Bootless speed,
When cowardice pursues and valour flies!

DEMETRIUS.
I will not stay thy questions. Let me go,
Or if thou follow me, do not believe
But I shall do thee mischief in the wood.

HELENA.
Ay, in the temple, in the town, the field,
You do me mischief. Fie, Demetrius!
Your wrongs do set a scandal on my sex.
We cannot fight for love as men may do.
We should be woo'd, and were not made to woo.

[*Exit Demetrius.*]

I'll follow thee, and make a heaven of hell,
To die upon the hand I love so well.

[*Exit Helena.*]

OBERON.
Fare thee well, nymph. Ere he do leave this grove,
Thou shalt fly him, and he shall seek thy love.

Enter Puck.

Hast thou the flower there? Welcome, wanderer.

PUCK.
Ay, there it is.

22

OBERON.
I pray thee give it me.
I know a bank where the wild thyme blows,
Where oxlips and the nodding violet grows,
Quite over-canopied with luscious woodbine,
With sweet musk-roses, and with eglantine.
There sleeps Titania sometime of the night,
Lull'd in these flowers with dances and delight;
And there the snake throws her enamell'd skin,
Weed wide enough to wrap a fairy in.
And with the juice of this I'll streak her eyes,
And make her full of hateful fantasies.
Take thou some of it, and seek through this grove:
A sweet Athenian lady is in love
With a disdainful youth. Anoint his eyes;
But do it when the next thing he espies
May be the lady. Thou shalt know the man
By the Athenian garments he hath on.
Effect it with some care, that he may prove
More fond on her than she upon her love:
And look thou meet me ere the first cock crow.

PUCK.
Fear not, my lord, your servant shall do so.

[*Exeunt.*]

SCENE II

Another part of the wood

Enter Titania with her Train.

TITANIA.
Come, now a roundel and a fairy song;
Then for the third part of a minute, hence;
Some to kill cankers in the musk-rose buds;
Some war with reremice for their leathern wings,
To make my small elves coats; and some keep back
The clamorous owl, that nightly hoots and wonders
At our quaint spirits. Sing me now asleep;
Then to your offices, and let me rest.

Fairies sing.

FIRST FAIRY.
  You spotted snakes with double tongue,
    Thorny hedgehogs, be not seen;
  Newts and blind-worms do no wrong,
    Come not near our Fairy Queen:

CHORUS.
  Philomel, with melody,
  Sing in our sweet lullaby:
Lulla, lulla, lullaby; lulla, lulla, lullaby.
  Never harm, nor spell, nor charm,
  Come our lovely lady nigh;
  So good night, with lullaby.

FIRST FAIRY.
  Weaving spiders, come not here;
    Hence, you long-legg'd spinners, hence.
  Beetles black, approach not near;
    Worm nor snail do no offence.

24

CHORUS.
Philomel with melody, &c.

SECOND FAIRY.
Hence away! Now all is well.
One aloof stand sentinel.

[*Exeunt Fairies. Titania sleeps.*]

Enter Oberon.

OBERON.
What thou seest when thou dost wake,

[*Squeezes the flower on Titania's eyelids.*]

Do it for thy true love take;
Love and languish for his sake.
Be it ounce, or cat, or bear,
Pard, or boar with bristled hair,
In thy eye that shall appear
When thou wak'st, it is thy dear.
Wake when some vile thing is near.

[*Exit.*]

Enter Lysander and Hermia.

LYSANDER.
Fair love, you faint with wand'ring in the wood.
And, to speak troth, I have forgot our way.
We'll rest us, Hermia, if you think it good,
And tarry for the comfort of the day.

HERMIA.
Be it so, Lysander: find you out a bed,
For I upon this bank will rest my head.

LYSANDER.
One turf shall serve as pillow for us both;
One heart, one bed, two bosoms, and one troth.

HERMIA.
Nay, good Lysander; for my sake, my dear,
Lie further off yet, do not lie so near.

LYSANDER.
O take the sense, sweet, of my innocence!
Love takes the meaning in love's conference.
I mean that my heart unto yours is knit,
So that but one heart we can make of it:
Two bosoms interchainèd with an oath,
So then two bosoms and a single troth.
Then by your side no bed-room me deny;
For lying so, Hermia, I do not lie.

HERMIA.
Lysander riddles very prettily.
Now much beshrew my manners and my pride,
If Hermia meant to say Lysander lied!
But, gentle friend, for love and courtesy
Lie further off, in human modesty,
Such separation as may well be said
Becomes a virtuous bachelor and a maid,
So far be distant; and good night, sweet friend:
Thy love ne'er alter till thy sweet life end!

LYSANDER.
Amen, amen, to that fair prayer say I;
And then end life when I end loyalty!
Here is my bed. Sleep give thee all his rest!

HERMIA.
With half that wish the wisher's eyes be pressed!

[*They sleep.*]

Enter Puck.

PUCK.
Through the forest have I gone,
But Athenian found I none,
On whose eyes I might approve
This flower's force in stirring love.
Night and silence! Who is here?
Weeds of Athens he doth wear:
This is he, my master said,
Despisèd the Athenian maid;
And here the maiden, sleeping sound,
On the dank and dirty ground.
Pretty soul, she durst not lie

Near this lack-love, this kill-courtesy.
Churl, upon thy eyes I throw
All the power this charm doth owe;
When thou wak'st let love forbid
Sleep his seat on thy eyelid.
So awake when I am gone;
For I must now to Oberon.

[Exit.]

Enter Demetrius and Helena, running.

HELENA.
Stay, though thou kill me, sweet Demetrius.

DEMETRIUS.
I charge thee, hence, and do not haunt me thus.

HELENA.
O, wilt thou darkling leave me? Do not so.

DEMETRIUS.
Stay, on thy peril; I alone will go.

[Exit Demetrius.]

HELENA.
O, I am out of breath in this fond chase!
The more my prayer, the lesser is my grace.
Happy is Hermia, wheresoe'er she lies,
For she hath blessèd and attractive eyes.
How came her eyes so bright? Not with salt tears.
If so, my eyes are oftener wash'd than hers.
No, no, I am as ugly as a bear,
For beasts that meet me run away for fear:
Therefore no marvel though Demetrius
Do, as a monster, fly my presence thus.
What wicked and dissembling glass of mine
Made me compare with Hermia's sphery eyne?
But who is here? Lysander, on the ground!
Dead or asleep? I see no blood, no wound.
Lysander, if you live, good sir, awake.

LYSANDER.
[*Waking.*] And run through fire I will for thy sweet sake.

Transparent Helena! Nature shows art,
That through thy bosom makes me see thy heart.
Where is Demetrius? O, how fit a word
Is that vile name to perish on my sword!

HELENA.
Do not say so, Lysander, say not so.
What though he love your Hermia? Lord, what though?
Yet Hermia still loves you. Then be content.

LYSANDER.
Content with Hermia? No, I do repent
The tedious minutes I with her have spent.
Not Hermia, but Helena I love.
Who will not change a raven for a dove?
The will of man is by his reason sway'd,
And reason says you are the worthier maid.
Things growing are not ripe until their season;
So I, being young, till now ripe not to reason;
And touching now the point of human skill,
Reason becomes the marshal to my will,
And leads me to your eyes, where I o'erlook
Love's stories, written in love's richest book.

HELENA.
Wherefore was I to this keen mockery born?
When at your hands did I deserve this scorn?
Is't not enough, is't not enough, young man,
That I did never, no, nor never can
Deserve a sweet look from Demetrius' eye,
But you must flout my insufficiency?
Good troth, you do me wrong, good sooth, you do,
In such disdainful manner me to woo.
But fare you well; perforce I must confess,
I thought you lord of more true gentleness.
O, that a lady of one man refus'd,
Should of another therefore be abus'd!

[*Exit.*]

LYSANDER.
She sees not Hermia. Hermia, sleep thou there,
And never mayst thou come Lysander near!
For, as a surfeit of the sweetest things
The deepest loathing to the stomach brings;

Or as the heresies that men do leave
Are hated most of those they did deceive;
So thou, my surfeit and my heresy,
Of all be hated, but the most of me!
And, all my powers, address your love and might
To honour Helen, and to be her knight!

[*Exit.*]

HERMIA.
[*Starting.*] Help me, Lysander, help me! Do thy best
To pluck this crawling serpent from my breast!
Ay me, for pity! What a dream was here!
Lysander, look how I do quake with fear.
Methought a serpent eat my heart away,
And you sat smiling at his cruel prey.
Lysander! What, removed? Lysander! lord!
What, out of hearing? Gone? No sound, no word?
Alack, where are you? Speak, and if you hear;
Speak, of all loves! I swoon almost with fear.
No? Then I well perceive you are not nigh.
Either death or you I'll find immediately.

[*Exit.*]

ACT III

SCENE I

The Wood

The Queen of Fairies still lying asleep.

Enter Bottom, Quince, Snout, Starveling, Snug and Flute.

BOTTOM.
Are we all met?

QUINCE.
Pat, pat; and here's a marvellous convenient place for our rehearsal. This green plot shall be our stage, this hawthorn brake our tiring-house; and we will do it in action, as we will do it before the Duke.

BOTTOM.
Peter Quince?

QUINCE.
What sayest thou, bully Bottom?

BOTTOM.
There are things in this comedy of Pyramus and Thisbe that will never please. First, Pyramus must draw a sword to kill himself; which the ladies cannot abide. How answer you that?

SNOUT
By'r lakin, a parlous fear.

STARVELING.
I believe we must leave the killing out, when all is done.

30

BOTTOM.
Not a whit; I have a device to make all well. Write me a prologue, and let the prologue seem to say we will do no harm with our swords, and that Pyramus is not killed indeed; and for the more better assurance, tell them that I Pyramus am not Pyramus but Bottom the weaver. This will put them out of fear.

QUINCE.
Well, we will have such a prologue; and it shall be written in eight and six.

BOTTOM.
No, make it two more; let it be written in eight and eight.

SNOUT
Will not the ladies be afeard of the lion?

STARVELING.
I fear it, I promise you.

BOTTOM.
Masters, you ought to consider with yourselves, to bring in (God shield us!) a lion among ladies is a most dreadful thing. For there is not a more fearful wild-fowl than your lion living; and we ought to look to it.

SNOUT
Therefore another prologue must tell he is not a lion.

BOTTOM.
Nay, you must name his name, and half his face must be seen through the lion's neck; and he himself must speak through, saying thus, or to the same defect: 'Ladies,' or, 'Fair ladies, I would wish you,' or, 'I would request you,' or, 'I would entreat you, not to fear, not to tremble: my life for yours. If you think I come hither as a lion, it were pity of my life. No, I am no such thing; I am a man as other men are': and there, indeed, let him name his name, and tell them plainly he is Snug the joiner.

QUINCE.
Well, it shall be so. But there is two hard things: that is, to bring the moonlight into a chamber, for you know, Pyramus and Thisbe meet by moonlight.

SNOUT
Doth the moon shine that night we play our play?

BOTTOM.
A calendar, a calendar! Look in the almanack; find out moonshine, find out moonshine.

QUINCE.
Yes, it doth shine that night.

BOTTOM.
Why, then may you leave a casement of the great chamber window, where we play, open; and the moon may shine in at the casement.

QUINCE.
Ay; or else one must come in with a bush of thorns and a lantern, and say he comes to disfigure or to present the person of Moonshine. Then there is another thing: we must have a wall in the great chamber; for Pyramus and Thisbe, says the story, did talk through the chink of a wall.

SNOUT
You can never bring in a wall. What say you, Bottom?

BOTTOM.
Some man or other must present Wall. And let him have some plaster, or some loam, or some rough-cast about him, to signify wall; and let him hold his fingers thus, and through that cranny shall Pyramus and Thisbe whisper.

QUINCE.
If that may be, then all is well. Come, sit down, every mother's son, and rehearse your parts. Pyramus, you begin: when you have spoken your speech, enter into that brake; and so everyone according to his cue.

Enter Puck behind.

PUCK.
What hempen homespuns have we swaggering here,
So near the cradle of the Fairy Queen?
What, a play toward? I'll be an auditor;
An actor too perhaps, if I see cause.

QUINCE.
Speak, Pyramus.—Thisbe, stand forth.

PYRAMUS.
Thisbe, the flowers of odious savours sweet

32

QUINCE.
Odours, odours.

PYRAMUS.
. . . *odours savours sweet.*
So hath thy breath, my dearest Thisbe dear.
But hark, a voice! Stay thou but here awhile,
And by and by I will to thee appear.

[*Exit.*]

PUCK.
A stranger Pyramus than e'er played here!

[*Exit.*]

THISBE.
Must I speak now?

QUINCE.
Ay, marry, must you, For you must understand he goes but to see a
noise that he heard, and is to come again.

THISBE.
Most radiant Pyramus, most lily-white of hue,
Of colour like the red rose on triumphant brier,
Most brisky juvenal, and eke most lovely Jew,
As true as truest horse, that yet would never tire,
I'll meet thee, Pyramus, at Ninny's tomb.

QUINCE.
Ninus' tomb, man! Why, you must not speak that yet. That you
answer to Pyramus. You speak all your part at once, cues, and all.—
Pyramus enter! Your cue is past; it is 'never tire.'

THISBE.
O, *As true as truest horse, that yet would never tire.*

Enter Puck and Bottom with an ass's head.

PYRAMUS.
If I were fair, Thisbe, I were only thine.

QUINCE.
O monstrous! O strange! We are haunted. Pray, masters, fly,
masters! Help!

[Exeunt Clowns.]

PUCK.
I'll follow you. I'll lead you about a round,
  Through bog, through bush, through brake, through brier;
Sometime a horse I'll be, sometime a hound,
  A hog, a headless bear, sometime a fire;
And neigh, and bark, and grunt, and roar, and burn,
Like horse, hound, hog, bear, fire, at every turn.

[Exit.]

BOTTOM.
Why do they run away? This is a knavery of them to make me afeard.

Enter Snout.

SNOUT
O Bottom, thou art changed! What do I see on thee?

BOTTOM.
What do you see? You see an ass-head of your own, do you?

[Exit Snout.]

Enter Quince.

QUINCE.
Bless thee, Bottom! bless thee! Thou art translated.

[Exit.]

BOTTOM.
I see their knavery. This is to make an ass of me, to fright me, if they could. But I will not stir from this place, do what they can. I will walk up and down here, and I will sing, that they shall hear I am not afraid.
[*Sings.*]
    The ousel cock, so black of hue,
      With orange-tawny bill,
    The throstle with his note so true,
      The wren with little quill.

TITANIA.
[*Waking.*] What angel wakes me from my flowery bed?

34

BOTTOM.
[*Sings.*]
> The finch, the sparrow, and the lark,
>   The plain-song cuckoo gray,
> Whose note full many a man doth mark,
>   And dares not answer nay.

for, indeed, who would set his wit to so foolish a bird? Who would give a bird the lie, though he cry 'cuckoo' never so?

TITANIA.
I pray thee, gentle mortal, sing again.
Mine ear is much enamour'd of thy note.
So is mine eye enthrallèd to thy shape;
And thy fair virtue's force perforce doth move me,
On the first view, to say, to swear, I love thee.

BOTTOM.
Methinks, mistress, you should have little reason for that. And yet, to say the truth, reason and love keep little company together nowadays. The more the pity that some honest neighbours will not make them friends. Nay, I can gleek upon occasion.

TITANIA.
Thou art as wise as thou art beautiful.

BOTTOM.
Not so, neither; but if I had wit enough to get out of this wood, I have enough to serve mine own turn.

TITANIA.
Out of this wood do not desire to go.
Thou shalt remain here whether thou wilt or no.
I am a spirit of no common rate.
The summer still doth tend upon my state;
And I do love thee: therefore, go with me.
I'll give thee fairies to attend on thee;
And they shall fetch thee jewels from the deep,
And sing, while thou on pressèd flowers dost sleep.
And I will purge thy mortal grossness so
That thou shalt like an airy spirit go.—
Peaseblossom! Cobweb! Moth! and Mustardseed!

Enter four Fairies.

35

PEASEBLOSSOM.
Ready.

COBWEB.
And I.

MOTH.
And I.

MUSTARDSEED.
And I.

ALL.
Where shall we go?

TITANIA.
Be kind and courteous to this gentleman;
Hop in his walks and gambol in his eyes;
Feed him with apricocks and dewberries,
With purple grapes, green figs, and mulberries;
The honey-bags steal from the humble-bees,
And for night-tapers, crop their waxen thighs,
And light them at the fiery glow-worm's eyes,
To have my love to bed and to arise;
And pluck the wings from painted butterflies,
To fan the moonbeams from his sleeping eyes.
Nod to him, elves, and do him courtesies.

PEASEBLOSSOM.
Hail, mortal!

COBWEB.
Hail!

MOTH.
Hail!

MUSTARDSEED.
Hail!

BOTTOM.
I cry your worships mercy, heartily.—I beseech your worship's
name.

COBWEB.
Cobweb.

36

BOTTOM.
I shall desire you of more acquaintance, good Master Cobweb. If I
cut my finger, I shall make bold with you.—Your name, honest
gentleman?

PEASEBLOSSOM.
Peaseblossom.

BOTTOM.
I pray you, commend me to Mistress Squash, your mother, and to
Master Peascod, your father. Good Master Peaseblossom, I shall
desire you of more acquaintance too.—Your name, I beseech you,
sir?

MUSTARDSEED.
Mustardseed.

BOTTOM.
Good Master Mustardseed, I know your patience well. That same
cowardly giant-like ox-beef hath devoured many a gentleman of
your house. I promise you, your kindred hath made my eyes water
ere now. I desire you of more acquaintance, good Master
Mustardseed.

TITANIA.
Come, wait upon him; lead him to my bower.
   The moon, methinks, looks with a watery eye,
And when she weeps, weeps every little flower,
   Lamenting some enforced chastity.
Tie up my love's tongue, bring him silently.

[*Exeunt.*]

SCENE II

Another part of the wood

Enter Oberon.

OBERON.
I wonder if Titania be awak'd;
Then, what it was that next came in her eye,
Which she must dote on in extremity.

Enter Puck.

Here comes my messenger. How now, mad spirit?
What night-rule now about this haunted grove?

PUCK.
My mistress with a monster is in love.
Near to her close and consecrated bower,
While she was in her dull and sleeping hour,
A crew of patches, rude mechanicals,
That work for bread upon Athenian stalls,
Were met together to rehearse a play
Intended for great Theseus' nuptial day.
The shallowest thick-skin of that barren sort
Who Pyramus presented in their sport,
Forsook his scene and enter'd in a brake.
When I did him at this advantage take,
An ass's nole I fixed on his head.
Anon, his Thisbe must be answerèd,
And forth my mimic comes. When they him spy,
As wild geese that the creeping fowler eye,
Or russet-pated choughs, many in sort,
Rising and cawing at the gun's report,
Sever themselves and madly sweep the sky,
So at his sight away his fellows fly,
And at our stamp, here o'er and o'er one falls;
He murder cries, and help from Athens calls.

Their sense thus weak, lost with their fears, thus strong,
Made senseless things begin to do them wrong;
For briers and thorns at their apparel snatch;
Some sleeves, some hats, from yielders all things catch.
I led them on in this distracted fear,
And left sweet Pyramus translated there.
When in that moment, so it came to pass,
Titania wak'd, and straightway lov'd an ass.

OBERON.
This falls out better than I could devise.
But hast thou yet latch'd the Athenian's eyes
With the love-juice, as I did bid thee do?

PUCK.
I took him sleeping—that is finish'd too—
And the Athenian woman by his side,
That, when he wak'd, of force she must be ey'd.

Enter Demetrius and Hermia.

OBERON.
Stand close. This is the same Athenian.

PUCK.
This is the woman, but not this the man.

DEMETRIUS.
O why rebuke you him that loves you so?
Lay breath so bitter on your bitter foe.

HERMIA.
Now I but chide, but I should use thee worse,
For thou, I fear, hast given me cause to curse.
If thou hast slain Lysander in his sleep,
Being o'er shoes in blood, plunge in the deep,
And kill me too.
The sun was not so true unto the day
As he to me. Would he have stol'n away
From sleeping Hermia? I'll believe as soon
This whole earth may be bor'd, and that the moon
May through the centre creep and so displease
Her brother's noontide with th' Antipodes.
It cannot be but thou hast murder'd him.
So should a murderer look, so dead, so grim.

DEMETRIUS.
So should the murder'd look, and so should I,
Pierc'd through the heart with your stern cruelty.
Yet you, the murderer, look as bright, as clear,
As yonder Venus in her glimmering sphere.

HERMIA.
What's this to my Lysander? Where is he?
Ah, good Demetrius, wilt thou give him me?

DEMETRIUS.
I had rather give his carcass to my hounds.

HERMIA.
Out, dog! Out, cur! Thou driv'st me past the bounds
Of maiden's patience. Hast thou slain him, then?
Henceforth be never number'd among men!
O once tell true; tell true, even for my sake!
Durst thou have look'd upon him, being awake,
And hast thou kill'd him sleeping? O brave touch!
Could not a worm, an adder, do so much?
An adder did it; for with doubler tongue
Than thine, thou serpent, never adder stung.

DEMETRIUS.
You spend your passion on a mispris'd mood:
I am not guilty of Lysander's blood;
Nor is he dead, for aught that I can tell.

HERMIA.
I pray thee, tell me then that he is well.

DEMETRIUS.
And if I could, what should I get therefore?

HERMIA.
A privilege never to see me more.
And from thy hated presence part I so:
See me no more, whether he be dead or no.

[*Exit.*]

DEMETRIUS.
There is no following her in this fierce vein.
Here, therefore, for a while I will remain.

So sorrow's heaviness doth heavier grow
For debt that bankrupt sleep doth sorrow owe;
Which now in some slight measure it will pay,
If for his tender here I make some stay.

[*Lies down.*]

OBERON.
What hast thou done? Thou hast mistaken quite,
And laid the love-juice on some true-love's sight.
Of thy misprision must perforce ensue
Some true love turn'd, and not a false turn'd true.

PUCK.
Then fate o'er-rules, that, one man holding troth,
A million fail, confounding oath on oath.

OBERON.
About the wood go swifter than the wind,
And Helena of Athens look thou find.
All fancy-sick she is, and pale of cheer
With sighs of love, that costs the fresh blood dear.
By some illusion see thou bring her here;
I'll charm his eyes against she do appear.

PUCK.
I go, I go; look how I go,
Swifter than arrow from the Tartar's bow.

[*Exit.*]

OBERON.
   Flower of this purple dye,
   Hit with Cupid's archery,
   Sink in apple of his eye.
   When his love he doth espy,
   Let her shine as gloriously
   As the Venus of the sky.—
   When thou wak'st, if she be by,
   Beg of her for remedy.

Enter Puck.

PUCK.
   Captain of our fairy band,
   Helena is here at hand,

And the youth mistook by me,
Pleading for a lover's fee.
Shall we their fond pageant see?
Lord, what fools these mortals be!

OBERON.
    Stand aside. The noise they make
    Will cause Demetrius to awake.

PUCK.
    Then will two at once woo one.
    That must needs be sport alone;
    And those things do best please me
    That befall prepost'rously.

Enter Lysander and Helena.

LYSANDER.
Why should you think that I should woo in scorn?
Scorn and derision never come in tears.
Look when I vow, I weep; and vows so born,
In their nativity all truth appears.
How can these things in me seem scorn to you,
Bearing the badge of faith, to prove them true?

HELENA.
You do advance your cunning more and more.
When truth kills truth, O devilish-holy fray!
These vows are Hermia's: will you give her o'er?
Weigh oath with oath, and you will nothing weigh:
Your vows to her and me, put in two scales,
Will even weigh; and both as light as tales.

LYSANDER.
I had no judgment when to her I swore.

HELENA.
Nor none, in my mind, now you give her o'er.

LYSANDER.
Demetrius loves her, and he loves not you.

DEMETRIUS.
[*Waking.*] O Helen, goddess, nymph, perfect, divine!
To what, my love, shall I compare thine eyne?

42

Crystal is muddy. O how ripe in show
Thy lips, those kissing cherries, tempting grow!
That pure congealèd white, high Taurus' snow,
Fann'd with the eastern wind, turns to a crow
When thou hold'st up thy hand. O, let me kiss
This princess of pure white, this seal of bliss!

HELENA.
O spite! O hell! I see you all are bent
To set against me for your merriment.
If you were civil, and knew courtesy,
You would not do me thus much injury.
Can you not hate me, as I know you do,
But you must join in souls to mock me too?
If you were men, as men you are in show,
You would not use a gentle lady so;
To vow, and swear, and superpraise my parts,
When I am sure you hate me with your hearts.
You both are rivals, and love Hermia;
And now both rivals, to mock Helena.
A trim exploit, a manly enterprise,
To conjure tears up in a poor maid's eyes
With your derision! None of noble sort
Would so offend a virgin, and extort
A poor soul's patience, all to make you sport.

LYSANDER.
You are unkind, Demetrius; be not so,
For you love Hermia; this you know I know.
And here, with all good will, with all my heart,
In Hermia's love I yield you up my part;
And yours of Helena to me bequeath,
Whom I do love and will do till my death.

HELENA.
Never did mockers waste more idle breath.

DEMETRIUS.
Lysander, keep thy Hermia; I will none.
If e'er I lov'd her, all that love is gone.
My heart to her but as guest-wise sojourn'd;
And now to Helen is it home return'd,
There to remain.

LYSANDER.
Helen, it is not so.

43

DEMETRIUS.
Disparage not the faith thou dost not know,
Lest to thy peril thou aby it dear.
Look where thy love comes; yonder is thy dear.

Enter Hermia.

HERMIA.
Dark night, that from the eye his function takes,
The ear more quick of apprehension makes;
Wherein it doth impair the seeing sense,
It pays the hearing double recompense.
Thou art not by mine eye, Lysander, found;
Mine ear, I thank it, brought me to thy sound.
But why unkindly didst thou leave me so?

LYSANDER.
Why should he stay whom love doth press to go?

HERMIA.
What love could press Lysander from my side?

LYSANDER.
Lysander's love, that would not let him bide,
Fair Helena, who more engilds the night
Than all yon fiery oes and eyes of light.
Why seek'st thou me? Could not this make thee know
The hate I bare thee made me leave thee so?

HERMIA.
You speak not as you think; it cannot be.

HELENA.
Lo, she is one of this confederacy!
Now I perceive they have conjoin'd all three
To fashion this false sport in spite of me.
Injurious Hermia, most ungrateful maid!
Have you conspir'd, have you with these contriv'd,
To bait me with this foul derision?
Is all the counsel that we two have shar'd,
The sisters' vows, the hours that we have spent,
When we have chid the hasty-footed time
For parting us—O, is all forgot?
All school-days' friendship, childhood innocence?
We, Hermia, like two artificial gods,

44

Have with our needles created both one flower,
Both on one sampler, sitting on one cushion,
Both warbling of one song, both in one key,
As if our hands, our sides, voices, and minds,
Had been incorporate. So we grew together,
Like to a double cherry, seeming parted,
But yet a union in partition,
Two lovely berries moulded on one stem;
So, with two seeming bodies, but one heart;
Two of the first, like coats in heraldry,
Due but to one, and crownèd with one crest.
And will you rent our ancient love asunder,
To join with men in scorning your poor friend?
It is not friendly, 'tis not maidenly.
Our sex, as well as I, may chide you for it,
Though I alone do feel the injury.

HERMIA.
I am amazèd at your passionate words:
I scorn you not; it seems that you scorn me.

HELENA.
Have you not set Lysander, as in scorn,
To follow me, and praise my eyes and face?
And made your other love, Demetrius,
Who even but now did spurn me with his foot,
To call me goddess, nymph, divine and rare,
Precious, celestial? Wherefore speaks he this
To her he hates? And wherefore doth Lysander
Deny your love, so rich within his soul,
And tender me, forsooth, affection,
But by your setting on, by your consent?
What though I be not so in grace as you,
So hung upon with love, so fortunate,
But miserable most, to love unlov'd?
This you should pity rather than despise.

HERMIA.
I understand not what you mean by this.

HELENA.
Ay, do. Persever, counterfeit sad looks,
Make mouths upon me when I turn my back,
Wink each at other; hold the sweet jest up.
This sport, well carried, shall be chronicled.

If you have any pity, grace, or manners,
You would not make me such an argument.
But fare ye well. 'Tis partly my own fault,
Which death, or absence, soon shall remedy.

LYSANDER.
Stay, gentle Helena; hear my excuse;
My love, my life, my soul, fair Helena!

HELENA.
O excellent!

HERMIA.
Sweet, do not scorn her so.

DEMETRIUS.
If she cannot entreat, I can compel.

LYSANDER.
Thou canst compel no more than she entreat;
Thy threats have no more strength than her weak prayers.
Helen, I love thee, by my life I do;
I swear by that which I will lose for thee
To prove him false that says I love thee not.

DEMETRIUS.
I say I love thee more than he can do.

LYSANDER.
If thou say so, withdraw, and prove it too.

DEMETRIUS.
Quick, come.

HERMIA.
Lysander, whereto tends all this?

LYSANDER.
Away, you Ethiope!

DEMETRIUS.
No, no. He will
Seem to break loose. Take on as you would follow,
But yet come not. You are a tame man, go!

46

LYSANDER.
Hang off, thou cat, thou burr! Vile thing, let loose,
Or I will shake thee from me like a serpent.

HERMIA.
Why are you grown so rude? What change is this,
Sweet love?

LYSANDER.
Thy love? Out, tawny Tartar, out!
Out, loathèd medicine! O hated potion, hence!

HERMIA.
Do you not jest?

HELENA.
Yes, sooth, and so do you.

LYSANDER.
Demetrius, I will keep my word with thee.

DEMETRIUS.
I would I had your bond; for I perceive
A weak bond holds you; I'll not trust your word.

LYSANDER.
What, should I hurt her, strike her, kill her dead?
Although I hate her, I'll not harm her so.

HERMIA.
What, can you do me greater harm than hate?
Hate me? Wherefore? O me! what news, my love?
Am not I Hermia? Are not you Lysander?
I am as fair now as I was erewhile.
Since night you lov'd me; yet since night you left me.
Why then, you left me—O, the gods forbid!—
In earnest, shall I say?

LYSANDER.
Ay, by my life;
And never did desire to see thee more.
Therefore be out of hope, of question, of doubt;
Be certain, nothing truer; 'tis no jest
That I do hate thee and love Helena.

HERMIA.
O me! You juggler! You cankerblossom!
You thief of love! What! have you come by night
And stol'n my love's heart from him?

HELENA.
Fine, i' faith!
Have you no modesty, no maiden shame,
No touch of bashfulness? What, will you tear
Impatient answers from my gentle tongue?
Fie, fie, you counterfeit, you puppet, you!

HERMIA.
Puppet! Why so? Ay, that way goes the game.
Now I perceive that she hath made compare
Between our statures; she hath urg'd her height;
And with her personage, her tall personage,
Her height, forsooth, she hath prevail'd with him.
And are you grown so high in his esteem
Because I am so dwarfish and so low?
How low am I, thou painted maypole? Speak,
How low am I? I am not yet so low
But that my nails can reach unto thine eyes.

HELENA.
I pray you, though you mock me, gentlemen,
Let her not hurt me. I was never curst;
I have no gift at all in shrewishness;
I am a right maid for my cowardice;
Let her not strike me. You perhaps may think,
Because she is something lower than myself,
That I can match her.

HERMIA.
Lower! Hark, again.

HELENA.
Good Hermia, do not be so bitter with me.
I evermore did love you, Hermia,
Did ever keep your counsels, never wrong'd you,
Save that, in love unto Demetrius,
I told him of your stealth unto this wood.
He follow'd you; for love I follow'd him;
But he hath chid me hence, and threaten'd me
To strike me, spurn me, nay, to kill me too:

And now, so you will let me quiet go,
To Athens will I bear my folly back,
And follow you no further. Let me go:
You see how simple and how fond I am.

HERMIA.
Why, get you gone. Who is't that hinders you?

HELENA.
A foolish heart that I leave here behind.

HERMIA.
What! with Lysander?

HELENA.
With Demetrius.

LYSANDER.
Be not afraid; she shall not harm thee, Helena.

DEMETRIUS.
No, sir, she shall not, though you take her part.

HELENA.
O, when she's angry, she is keen and shrewd.
She was a vixen when she went to school,
And though she be but little, she is fierce.

HERMIA.
Little again! Nothing but low and little?
Why will you suffer her to flout me thus?
Let me come to her.

LYSANDER.
Get you gone, you dwarf;
You minimus, of hind'ring knot-grass made;
You bead, you acorn.

DEMETRIUS.
You are too officious
In her behalf that scorns your services.
Let her alone. Speak not of Helena;
Take not her part; for if thou dost intend
Never so little show of love to her,
Thou shalt aby it.

LYSANDER.
Now she holds me not.
Now follow, if thou dar'st, to try whose right,
Of thine or mine, is most in Helena.

DEMETRIUS.
Follow! Nay, I'll go with thee, cheek by jole.

[Exeunt Lysander and Demetrius.]

HERMIA.
You, mistress, all this coil is long of you.
Nay, go not back.

HELENA.
I will not trust you, I,
Nor longer stay in your curst company.
Your hands than mine are quicker for a fray.
My legs are longer though, to run away.

[Exit.]

HERMIA.
I am amaz'd, and know not what to say.

[Exit, pursuing Helena.]

OBERON.
This is thy negligence: still thou mistak'st,
Or else commit'st thy knaveries willfully.

PUCK.
Believe me, king of shadows, I mistook.
Did not you tell me I should know the man
By the Athenian garments he had on?
And so far blameless proves my enterprise
That I have 'nointed an Athenian's eyes:
And so far am I glad it so did sort,
As this their jangling I esteem a sport.

OBERON.
Thou seest these lovers seek a place to fight.
Hie therefore, Robin, overcast the night;
The starry welkin cover thou anon
With drooping fog, as black as Acheron,
And lead these testy rivals so astray

As one come not within another's way.
Like to Lysander sometime frame thy tongue,
Then stir Demetrius up with bitter wrong;
And sometime rail thou like Demetrius.
And from each other look thou lead them thus,
Till o'er their brows death-counterfeiting sleep
With leaden legs and batty wings doth creep.
Then crush this herb into Lysander's eye,
Whose liquor hath this virtuous property,
To take from thence all error with his might
And make his eyeballs roll with wonted sight.
When they next wake, all this derision
Shall seem a dream and fruitless vision;
And back to Athens shall the lovers wend,
With league whose date till death shall never end.
Whiles I in this affair do thee employ,
I'll to my queen, and beg her Indian boy;
And then I will her charmèd eye release
From monster's view, and all things shall be peace.

PUCK.
My fairy lord, this must be done with haste,
For night's swift dragons cut the clouds full fast;
And yonder shines Aurora's harbinger,
At whose approach, ghosts wandering here and there
Troop home to churchyards. Damnèd spirits all,
That in cross-ways and floods have burial,
Already to their wormy beds are gone;
For fear lest day should look their shames upon,
They wilfully themselves exile from light,
And must for aye consort with black-brow'd night.

OBERON.
But we are spirits of another sort:
I with the morning's love have oft made sport;
And, like a forester, the groves may tread
Even till the eastern gate, all fiery-red,
Opening on Neptune with fair blessèd beams,
Turns into yellow gold his salt-green streams.
But, notwithstanding, haste, make no delay.
We may effect this business yet ere day.

[*Exit Oberon.*]

PUCK.
  Up and down, up and down,
  I will lead them up and down.
  I am fear'd in field and town.
  Goblin, lead them up and down.
Here comes one.

Enter Lysander.

LYSANDER.
Where art thou, proud Demetrius? Speak thou now.

PUCK.
Here, villain, drawn and ready. Where art thou?

LYSANDER.
I will be with thee straight.

PUCK.
Follow me then to plainer ground.

[*Exit Lysander as following the voice.*]

Enter Demetrius.

DEMETRIUS.
Lysander, speak again.
Thou runaway, thou coward, art thou fled?
Speak. In some bush? Where dost thou hide thy head?

PUCK.
Thou coward, art thou bragging to the stars,
Telling the bushes that thou look'st for wars,
And wilt not come? Come, recreant, come, thou child!
I'll whip thee with a rod. He is defil'd
That draws a sword on thee.

DEMETRIUS.
Yea, art thou there?

PUCK.
Follow my voice; we'll try no manhood here.

[*Exeunt.*]

Enter Lysander.

LYSANDER.
He goes before me, and still dares me on;
When I come where he calls, then he is gone.
The villain is much lighter-heel'd than I:
I follow'd fast, but faster he did fly,
That fallen am I in dark uneven way,
And here will rest me. Come, thou gentle day!
[*Lies down.*] For if but once thou show me thy grey light,
I'll find Demetrius, and revenge this spite.

[*Sleeps.*]

Enter Puck and Demetrius.

PUCK.
Ho, ho, ho! Coward, why com'st thou not?

DEMETRIUS.
Abide me, if thou dar'st; for well I wot
Thou runn'st before me, shifting every place,
And dar'st not stand, nor look me in the face.
Where art thou?

PUCK.
Come hither; I am here.

DEMETRIUS.
Nay, then, thou mock'st me. Thou shalt buy this dear
If ever I thy face by daylight see:
Now go thy way. Faintness constraineth me
To measure out my length on this cold bed.
By day's approach look to be visitcd.

[*Lies down and sleeps.*]

Enter Helena.

HELENA.
O weary night, O long and tedious night,
   Abate thy hours! Shine, comforts, from the east,
That I may back to Athens by daylight,
   From these that my poor company detest.
And sleep, that sometimes shuts up sorrow's eye,
Steal me awhile from mine own company.

[*Sleeps.*]

PUCK.
  Yet but three? Come one more.
  Two of both kinds makes up four.
  Here she comes, curst and sad.
  Cupid is a knavish lad
  Thus to make poor females mad.

Enter Hermia.

HERMIA.
Never so weary, never so in woe,
  Bedabbled with the dew, and torn with briers,
I can no further crawl, no further go;
  My legs can keep no pace with my desires.
Here will I rest me till the break of day.
Heavens shield Lysander, if they mean a fray!

[*Lies down.*]

PUCK.
   On the ground
   Sleep sound.
   I'll apply
   To your eye,
  Gentle lover, remedy.

[*Squeezing the juice on Lysander's eye.*]

   When thou wak'st,
   Thou tak'st
   True delight
   In the sight
  Of thy former lady's eye.
  And the country proverb known,
  That every man should take his own,
  In your waking shall be shown:
   Jack shall have Jill;
   Nought shall go ill;
The man shall have his mare again, and all shall be well.

[*Exit Puck.*]

ACT IV

SCENE I

The Wood

Lysander, Demetrius, Helena and Hermia still asleep.

Enter Titania and Bottom; Peaseblossom, Cobweb, Moth, Mustardseed and other Fairies attending; Oberon behind, unseen.

TITANIA.
Come, sit thee down upon this flowery bed,
  While I thy amiable cheeks do coy,
And stick musk-roses in thy sleek smooth head,
  And kiss thy fair large ears, my gentle joy.

BOTTOM.
Where's Peaseblossom?

PEASEBLOSSOM.
Ready.

BOTTOM.
Scratch my head, Peaseblossom. Where's Monsieur Cobweb?

COBWEB.
Ready.

BOTTOM.
Monsieur Cobweb; good monsieur, get you your weapons in your hand and kill me a red-hipped humble-bee on the top of a thistle; and, good monsieur, bring me the honey-bag. Do not fret yourself too much in the action, monsieur; and, good monsieur, have a care the honey-bag break not; I would be loath to have you overflown with a honey-bag, signior. Where's Monsieur Mustardseed?

MUSTARDSEED.
Ready.

BOTTOM.
Give me your neaf, Monsieur Mustardseed. Pray you, leave your
courtesy, good monsieur.

MUSTARDSEED.
What's your will?

BOTTOM.
Nothing, good monsieur, but to help Cavalery Cobweb to scratch. I
must to the barber's, monsieur, for methinks I am marvellous hairy
about the face; and I am such a tender ass, if my hair do but tickle
me, I must scratch.

TITANIA.
What, wilt thou hear some music, my sweet love?

BOTTOM.
I have a reasonable good ear in music. Let us have the tongs and the
bones.

TITANIA.
Or say, sweet love, what thou desirest to eat.

BOTTOM.
Truly, a peck of provender; I could munch your good dry oats.
Methinks I have a great desire to a bottle of hay: good hay, sweet
hay, hath no fellow.

TITANIA.
I have a venturous fairy that shall seek
The squirrel's hoard, and fetch thee new nuts.

BOTTOM.
I had rather have a handful or two of dried peas. But, I pray you, let
none of your people stir me; I have an exposition of sleep come
upon me.

TITANIA.
Sleep thou, and I will wind thee in my arms.
Fairies, be gone, and be all ways away.
So doth the woodbine the sweet honeysuckle
Gently entwist, the female ivy so

Enrings the barky fingers of the elm.
O, how I love thee! How I dote on thee!

[*They sleep.*]

Oberon advances. Enter Puck.

OBERON.
Welcome, good Robin. Seest thou this sweet sight?
Her dotage now I do begin to pity.
For, meeting her of late behind the wood,
Seeking sweet favours for this hateful fool,
I did upbraid her and fall out with her:
For she his hairy temples then had rounded
With coronet of fresh and fragrant flowers;
And that same dew, which sometime on the buds
Was wont to swell like round and orient pearls,
Stood now within the pretty flouriets' eyes,
Like tears that did their own disgrace bewail.
When I had at my pleasure taunted her,
And she in mild terms begg'd my patience,
I then did ask of her her changeling child;
Which straight she gave me, and her fairy sent
To bear him to my bower in fairyland.
And now I have the boy, I will undo
This hateful imperfection of her eyes.
And, gentle Puck, take this transformèd scalp
From off the head of this Athenian swain,
That he awaking when the other do,
May all to Athens back again repair,
And think no more of this night's accidents
But as the fierce vexation of a dream.
But first I will release the Fairy Queen.

[*Touching her eyes with an herb.*]

  Be as thou wast wont to be;
  See as thou was wont to see.
  Dian's bud o'er Cupid's flower
  Hath such force and blessed power.
Now, my Titania, wake you, my sweet queen.

TITANIA.
My Oberon, what visions have I seen!
Methought I was enamour'd of an ass.

OBERON.
There lies your love.

TITANIA.
How came these things to pass?
O, how mine eyes do loathe his visage now!

OBERON.
Silence awhile.—Robin, take off this head.
Titania, music call; and strike more dead
Than common sleep, of all these five the sense.

TITANIA.
Music, ho, music, such as charmeth sleep.

PUCK.
Now when thou wak'st, with thine own fool's eyes peep.

OBERON.
Sound, music.

[*Still mucic.*]

Come, my queen, take hands with me,
And rock the ground whereon these sleepers be.
Now thou and I are new in amity,
And will tomorrow midnight solemnly
Dance in Duke Theseus' house triumphantly,
And bless it to all fair prosperity:
There shall the pairs of faithful lovers be
Wedded, with Theseus, all in jollity.

PUCK.
  Fairy king, attend and mark.
  I do hear the morning lark.

OBERON.
  Then, my queen, in silence sad,
  Trip we after night's shade.
  We the globe can compass soon,
  Swifter than the wand'ring moon.

TITANIA.
  Come, my lord, and in our flight,
  Tell me how it came this night

That I sleeping here was found
With these mortals on the ground.

[Exeunt. Horns sound within.]

Enter Theseus, Hippolyta, Egeus and Train.

THESEUS.
Go, one of you, find out the forester;
For now our observation is perform'd;
And since we have the vaward of the day,
My love shall hear the music of my hounds.
Uncouple in the western valley; let them go.
Dispatch I say, and find the forester.

[Exit an Attendant.]

We will, fair queen, up to the mountain's top,
And mark the musical confusion
Of hounds and echo in conjunction.

HIPPOLYTA.
I was with Hercules and Cadmus once,
When in a wood of Crete they bay'd the bear
With hounds of Sparta. Never did I hear
Such gallant chiding; for, besides the groves,
The skies, the fountains, every region near
Seem'd all one mutual cry. I never heard
So musical a discord, such sweet thunder.

THESEUS.
My hounds are bred out of the Spartan kind,
So flew'd, so sanded; and their heads are hung
With ears that sweep away the morning dew;
Crook-knee'd and dewlap'd like Thessalian bulls;
Slow in pursuit, but match'd in mouth like bells,
Each under each. A cry more tuneable
Was never holla'd to, nor cheer'd with horn,
In Crete, in Sparta, nor in Thessaly.
Judge when you hear.—But, soft, what nymphs are these?

EGEUS.
My lord, this is my daughter here asleep,
And this Lysander; this Demetrius is;
This Helena, old Nedar's Helena:
I wonder of their being here together.

THESEUS.
No doubt they rose up early to observe
The rite of May; and, hearing our intent,
Came here in grace of our solemnity.
But speak, Egeus; is not this the day
That Hermia should give answer of her choice?

EGEUS.
It is, my lord.

THESEUS.
Go, bid the huntsmen wake them with their horns.

Horns, and shout within. Demetrius, Lysander, Hermia and Helena
wake and start up.

Good morrow, friends. Saint Valentine is past.
Begin these wood-birds but to couple now?

LYSANDER.
Pardon, my lord.

He and the rest kneel to Theseus.

THESEUS.
I pray you all, stand up.
I know you two are rival enemies.
How comes this gentle concord in the world,
That hatred is so far from jealousy
To sleep by hate, and fear no enmity?

LYSANDER.
My lord, I shall reply amazedly,
Half sleep, half waking; but as yet, I swear,
I cannot truly say how I came here.
But, as I think (for truly would I speak)
And now I do bethink me, so it is:
I came with Hermia hither. Our intent
Was to be gone from Athens, where we might be,
Without the peril of the Athenian law.

EGEUS.
Enough, enough, my lord; you have enough.
I beg the law, the law upon his head.
They would have stol'n away, they would, Demetrius,

Thereby to have defeated you and me:
You of your wife, and me of my consent,
Of my consent that she should be your wife.

DEMETRIUS.
My lord, fair Helen told me of their stealth,
Of this their purpose hither to this wood;
And I in fury hither follow'd them,
Fair Helena in fancy following me.
But, my good lord, I wot not by what power,
(But by some power it is) my love to Hermia,
Melted as the snow, seems to me now
As the remembrance of an idle gaud
Which in my childhood I did dote upon;
And all the faith, the virtue of my heart,
The object and the pleasure of mine eye,
Is only Helena. To her, my lord,
Was I betroth'd ere I saw Hermia.
But like a sickness did I loathe this food.
But, as in health, come to my natural taste,
Now I do wish it, love it, long for it,
And will for evermore be true to it.

THESEUS.
Fair lovers, you are fortunately met.
Of this discourse we more will hear anon.
Egeus, I will overbear your will;
For in the temple, by and by with us,
These couples shall eternally be knit.
And, for the morning now is something worn,
Our purpos'd hunting shall be set aside.
Away with us to Athens. Three and three,
We'll hold a feast in great solemnity.
Come, Hippolyta.

[*Exeunt Theseus, Hippolyta, Egeus and Train.*]

DEMETRIUS.
These things seem small and undistinguishable,
Like far-off mountains turnèd into clouds.

HERMIA.
Methinks I see these things with parted eye,
When everything seems double.

61

HELENA.
So methinks.
And I have found Demetrius like a jewel,
Mine own, and not mine own.

DEMETRIUS.
Are you sure
That we are awake? It seems to me
That yet we sleep, we dream. Do not you think
The Duke was here, and bid us follow him?

HERMIA.
Yea, and my father.

HELENA.
And Hippolyta.

LYSANDER.
And he did bid us follow to the temple.

DEMETRIUS.
Why, then, we are awake: let's follow him,
And by the way let us recount our dreams.

[*Exeunt.*]

BOTTOM.
[*Waking.*] When my cue comes, call me, and I will answer. My next
is 'Most fair Pyramus.' Heigh-ho! Peter Quince! Flute, the bellows-
mender! Snout, the tinker! Starveling! God's my life! Stol'n hence,
and left me asleep! I have had a most rare vision. I have had a
dream, past the wit of man to say what dream it was. Man is but an
ass if he go about to expound this dream. Methought I was—there is
no man can tell what. Methought I was, and methought I had—but
man is but a patched fool if he will offer to say what methought I
had. The eye of man hath not heard, the ear of man hath not seen,
man's hand is not able to taste, his tongue to conceive, nor his heart
to report, what my dream was. I will get Peter Quince to write a
ballad of this dream: it shall be called 'Bottom's Dream', because it
hath no bottom; and I will sing it in the latter end of a play, before
the Duke. Peradventure, to make it the more gracious, I shall sing it
at her death.

[*Exit.*]

SCENE II

Athens. A Room in Quince's House

Enter Quince, Flute, Snout and Starveling.

QUINCE.
Have you sent to Bottom's house? Is he come home yet?

STARVELING.
He cannot be heard of. Out of doubt he is transported.

FLUTE.
If he come not, then the play is marred. It goes not forward, doth it?

QUINCE.
It is not possible. You have not a man in all Athens able to discharge Pyramus but he.

FLUTE.
No, he hath simply the best wit of any handicraft man in Athens.

QUINCE.
Yea, and the best person too, and he is a very paramour for a sweet voice.

FLUTE.
You must say paragon. A paramour is, God bless us, a thing of naught.

Enter Snug.

SNUG
Masters, the Duke is coming from the temple, and there is two or three lords and ladies more married. If our sport had gone forward, we had all been made men.

FLUTE.
O sweet bully Bottom! Thus hath he lost sixpence a day during his life; he could not have 'scaped sixpence a day. An the Duke had not given him sixpence a day for playing Pyramus, I'll be hanged. He would have deserved it: sixpence a day in Pyramus, or nothing.

Enter Bottom.

BOTTOM.
Where are these lads? Where are these hearts?

QUINCE.
Bottom! O most courageous day! O most happy hour!

BOTTOM.
Masters, I am to discourse wonders: but ask me not what; for if I tell you, I am not true Athenian. I will tell you everything, right as it fell out.

QUINCE.
Let us hear, sweet Bottom.

BOTTOM.
Not a word of me. All that I will tell you is, that the Duke hath dined. Get your apparel together, good strings to your beards, new ribbons to your pumps; meet presently at the palace; every man look o'er his part. For the short and the long is, our play is preferred. In any case, let Thisbe have clean linen; and let not him that plays the lion pare his nails, for they shall hang out for the lion's claws. And most dear actors, eat no onions nor garlick, for we are to utter sweet breath; and I do not doubt but to hear them say it is a sweet comedy. No more words. Away! Go, away!

[*Exeunt.*]

ACT V

SCENE I

Athens. An Apartment in the Palace of Theseus

Enter Theseus, Hippolyta, Philostrate, Lords and Attendants.

HIPPOLYTA.
'Tis strange, my Theseus, that these lovers speak of.

THESEUS.
More strange than true. I never may believe
These antique fables, nor these fairy toys.
Lovers and madmen have such seething brains,
Such shaping fantasies, that apprehend
More than cool reason ever comprehends.
The lunatic, the lover, and the poet
Are of imagination all compact:
One sees more devils than vast hell can hold;
That is the madman: the lover, all as frantic,
Sees Helen's beauty in a brow of Egypt:
The poet's eye, in a fine frenzy rolling,
Doth glance from heaven to earth, from earth to heaven;
And as imagination bodies forth
The forms of things unknown, the poet's pen
Turns them to shapes, and gives to airy nothing
A local habitation and a name.
Such tricks hath strong imagination,
That if it would but apprehend some joy,
It comprehends some bringer of that joy.
Or in the night, imagining some fear,
How easy is a bush supposed a bear?

HIPPOLYTA.
But all the story of the night told over,
And all their minds transfigur'd so together,
More witnesseth than fancy's images,
And grows to something of great constancy;
But, howsoever, strange and admirable.

Enter lovers: Lysander, Demetrius, Hermia and Helena.

THESEUS.
Here come the lovers, full of joy and mirth.
Joy, gentle friends, joy and fresh days of love
Accompany your hearts!

LYSANDER.
More than to us
Wait in your royal walks, your board, your bed!

THESEUS.
Come now; what masques, what dances shall we have,
To wear away this long age of three hours
Between our after-supper and bed-time?
Where is our usual manager of mirth?
What revels are in hand? Is there no play
To ease the anguish of a torturing hour?
Call Philostrate.

PHILOSTRATE.
Here, mighty Theseus.

THESEUS.
Say, what abridgment have you for this evening?
What masque? What music? How shall we beguile
The lazy time, if not with some delight?

PHILOSTRATE.
There is a brief how many sports are ripe.
Make choice of which your Highness will see first.

[*Giving a paper.*]

THESEUS.
[*Reads*] 'The battle with the Centaurs, to be sung
By an Athenian eunuch to the harp.'
We'll none of that. That have I told my love

66

In glory of my kinsman Hercules.
'The riot of the tipsy Bacchanals,
Tearing the Thracian singer in their rage?'
That is an old device, and it was play'd
When I from Thebes came last a conqueror.
'The thrice three Muses mourning for the death
Of learning, late deceas'd in beggary.'
That is some satire, keen and critical,
Not sorting with a nuptial ceremony.
'A tedious brief scene of young Pyramus
And his love Thisbe; very tragical mirth.'
Merry and tragical? Tedious and brief?
That is hot ice and wondrous strange snow.
How shall we find the concord of this discord?

PHILOSTRATE.
A play there is, my lord, some ten words long,
Which is as brief as I have known a play;
But by ten words, my lord, it is too long,
Which makes it tedious. For in all the play
There is not one word apt, one player fitted.
And tragical, my noble lord, it is.
For Pyramus therein doth kill himself,
Which, when I saw rehears'd, I must confess,
Made mine eyes water; but more merry tears
The passion of loud laughter never shed.

THESEUS.
What are they that do play it?

PHILOSTRATE.
Hard-handed men that work in Athens here,
Which never labour'd in their minds till now;
And now have toil'd their unbreath'd memories
With this same play against your nuptial.

THESEUS.
And we will hear it.

PHILOSTRATE.
No, my noble lord,
It is not for you: I have heard it over,
And it is nothing, nothing in the world;
Unless you can find sport in their intents,

Extremely stretch'd and conn'd with cruel pain
To do you service.

THESEUS.
I will hear that play;
For never anything can be amiss
When simpleness and duty tender it.
Go, bring them in: and take your places, ladies.

[Exit Philostrate.]

HIPPOLYTA.
I love not to see wretchedness o'ercharged,
And duty in his service perishing.

THESEUS.
Why, gentle sweet, you shall see no such thing.

HIPPOLYTA.
He says they can do nothing in this kind.

THESEUS.
The kinder we, to give them thanks for nothing.
Our sport shall be to take what they mistake:
And what poor duty cannot do, noble respect
Takes it in might, not merit.
Where I have come, great clerks have purposed
To greet me with premeditated welcomes;
Where I have seen them shiver and look pale,
Make periods in the midst of sentences,
Throttle their practis'd accent in their fears,
And, in conclusion, dumbly have broke off,
Not paying me a welcome. Trust me, sweet,
Out of this silence yet I pick'd a welcome;
And in the modesty of fearful duty
I read as much as from the rattling tongue
Of saucy and audacious eloquence.
Love, therefore, and tongue-tied simplicity
In least speak most to my capacity.

Enter Philostrate.

PHILOSTRATE.
So please your grace, the Prologue is address'd.

THESEUS.
Let him approach.

Flourish of trumpets. Enter the Prologue.

PROLOGUE
If we offend, it is with our good will.
That you should think, we come not to offend,
But with good will. To show our simple skill,
That is the true beginning of our end.
Consider then, we come but in despite.
We do not come, as minding to content you,
Our true intent is. All for your delight
We are not here. That you should here repent you,
The actors are at hand, and, by their show,
You shall know all that you are like to know.

THESEUS.
This fellow doth not stand upon points.

LYSANDER.
He hath rid his prologue like a rough colt; he knows not the stop. A
good moral, my lord: it is not enough to speak, but to speak true.

HIPPOLYTA.
Indeed he hath played on this prologue like a child on a recorder; a
sound, but not in government.

THESEUS.
His speech was like a tangled chain; nothing impaired, but all
disordered. Who is next?

*Enter Pyramus and Thisbe, Wall, Moonshine and Lion as in dumb
show.*

PROLOGUE
Gentles, perchance you wonder at this show;
But wonder on, till truth make all things plain.
This man is Pyramus, if you would know;
This beauteous lady Thisbe is certain.
This man, with lime and rough-cast, doth present
Wall, that vile wall which did these lovers sunder;
And through Wall's chink, poor souls, they are content
To whisper, at the which let no man wonder.
This man, with lanthern, dog, and bush of thorn,

Presenteth Moonshine, for, if you will know,
By moonshine did these lovers think no scorn
To meet at Ninus' tomb, there, there to woo.
This grisly beast (which Lion hight by name)
The trusty Thisbe, coming first by night,
Did scare away, or rather did affright;
And as she fled, her mantle she did fall;
Which Lion vile with bloody mouth did stain.
Anon comes Pyramus, sweet youth, and tall,
And finds his trusty Thisbe's mantle slain;
Whereat with blade, with bloody blameful blade,
He bravely broach'd his boiling bloody breast;
And Thisbe, tarrying in mulberry shade,
His dagger drew, and died. For all the rest,
Let Lion, Moonshine, Wall, and lovers twain,
At large discourse while here they do remain.

[*Exeunt Prologue, Pyramus, Thisbe, Lion and Moonshine.*]

THESEUS.
I wonder if the lion be to speak.

DEMETRIUS.
No wonder, my lord. One lion may, when many asses do.

WALL.
In this same interlude it doth befall
That I, one Snout by name, present a wall:
And such a wall as I would have you think
That had in it a crannied hole or chink,
Through which the lovers, Pyramus and Thisbe,
Did whisper often very secretly.
This loam, this rough-cast, and this stone, doth show
That I am that same wall; the truth is so:
And this the cranny is, right and sinister,
Through which the fearful lovers are to whisper.

THESEUS.
Would you desire lime and hair to speak better?

DEMETRIUS.
It is the wittiest partition that ever I heard discourse, my lord.

THESEUS.
Pyramus draws near the wall; silence.

Enter Pyramus.

PYRAMUS.
O grim-look'd night! O night with hue so black!
O night, which ever art when day is not!
O night, O night, alack, alack, alack,
I fear my Thisbe's promise is forgot!
And thou, O wall, O sweet, O lovely wall,
That stand'st between her father's ground and mine;
Thou wall, O wall, O sweet and lovely wall,
Show me thy chink, to blink through with mine eyne.

[*Wall holds up his fingers.*]

Thanks, courteous wall: Jove shield thee well for this!
But what see I? No Thisbe do I see.
O wicked wall, through whom I see no bliss,
Curs'd be thy stones for thus deceiving me!

THESEUS.
The wall, methinks, being sensible, should curse again.

PYRAMUS.
No, in truth, sir, he should not. 'Deceiving me' is Thisbe's cue: she is
to enter now, and I am to spy her through the wall. You shall see it
will fall pat as I told you. Yonder she comes.

Enter Thisbe.

THISBE.
O wall, full often hast thou heard my moans,
For parting my fair Pyramus and me.
My cherry lips have often kiss'd thy stones,
Thy stones with lime and hair knit up in thee.

PYRAMUS.
I see a voice; now will I to the chink,
To spy an I can hear my Thisbe's face.
Thisbe?

THISBE.
My love thou art, my love I think.

PYRAMUS.
Think what thou wilt, I am thy lover's grace;
And like Limander am I trusty still.

71

THISBE.
And I like Helen, till the fates me kill.

PYRAMUS.
Not Shafalus to Procrus was so true.

THISBE.
As Shafalus to Procrus, I to you.

PYRAMUS.
O kiss me through the hole of this vile wall.

THISBE.
I kiss the wall's hole, not your lips at all.

PYRAMUS.
Wilt thou at Ninny's tomb meet me straightway?

THISBE.
'Tide life, 'tide death, I come without delay.

WALL.
Thus have I, Wall, my part discharged so;
And, being done, thus Wall away doth go.

[*Exeunt Wall, Pyramus and Thisbe.*]

THESEUS.
Now is the mural down between the two neighbours.

DEMETRIUS.
No remedy, my lord, when walls are so wilful to hear without
warning.

HIPPOLYTA.
This is the silliest stuff that ever I heard.

THESEUS.
The best in this kind are but shadows; and the worst are no worse, if
imagination amend them.

HIPPOLYTA.
It must be your imagination then, and not theirs.

THESEUS.
If we imagine no worse of them than they of themselves, they may

pass for excellent men. Here come two noble beasts in, a man and a lion.

Enter Lion and Moonshine.

LION.
You, ladies, you, whose gentle hearts do fear
The smallest monstrous mouse that creeps on floor,
May now, perchance, both quake and tremble here,
When lion rough in wildest rage doth roar.
Then know that I, one Snug the joiner, am
A lion fell, nor else no lion's dam;
For if I should as lion come in strife
Into this place, 'twere pity on my life.

THESEUS.
A very gentle beast, and of a good conscience.

DEMETRIUS.
The very best at a beast, my lord, that e'er I saw.

LYSANDER.
This lion is a very fox for his valour.

THESEUS.
True; and a goose for his discretion.

DEMETRIUS.
Not so, my lord, for his valour cannot carry his discretion, and the fox carries the goose.

THESEUS.
His discretion, I am sure, cannot carry his valour; for the goose carries not the fox. It is well; leave it to his discretion, and let us listen to the moon.

MOONSHINE.
This lanthorn doth the hornèd moon present.

DEMETRIUS.
He should have worn the horns on his head.

THESEUS.
He is no crescent, and his horns are invisible within the circumference.

73

MOONSHINE.
This lanthorn doth the hornèd moon present;
Myself the man i' the moon do seem to be.

THESEUS.
This is the greatest error of all the rest; the man should be put into the lantern. How is it else the man i' the moon?

DEMETRIUS.
He dares not come there for the candle, for you see, it is already in snuff.

HIPPOLYTA.
I am aweary of this moon. Would he would change!

THESEUS.
It appears by his small light of discretion that he is in the wane; but yet, in courtesy, in all reason, we must stay the time.

LYSANDER.
Proceed, Moon.

MOON
All that I have to say, is to tell you that the lantern is the moon; I the man i' the moon; this thorn-bush my thorn-bush; and this dog my dog.

DEMETRIUS.
Why, all these should be in the lantern, for all these are in the moon. But silence; here comes Thisbe.

Enter Thisbe.

THISBE.
This is old Ninny's tomb. Where is my love?

LION.
Oh!

[The Lion roars, Thisbe runs off.]

DEMETRIUS.
Well roared, Lion.

THESEUS.
Well run, Thisbe.

74

HIPPOLYTA.
Well shone, Moon. Truly, the moon shines with a good grace.

[*The Lion tears Thisbe's mantle, and exit.*]

THESEUS.
Well moused, Lion.

DEMETRIUS.
And then came Pyramus.

LYSANDER.
And so the lion vanished.

Enter Pyramus.

PYRAMUS.
Sweet Moon, I thank thee for thy sunny beams;
I thank thee, Moon, for shining now so bright;
For, by thy gracious golden, glittering gleams,
I trust to take of truest Thisbe sight.
　　　But stay! O spite!
　　　But mark, poor knight,
　　What dreadful dole is here!
　　　Eyes, do you see?
　　　How can it be?
　　O dainty duck! O dear!
　　　Thy mantle good,
　　　What, stained with blood?
　　Approach, ye Furies fell!
　　　O Fates, come, come;
　　　Cut thread and thrum;
　　Quail, rush, conclude, and quell!

THESEUS.
This passion, and the death of a dear friend, would go near to make
a man look sad.

HIPPOLYTA.
Beshrew my heart, but I pity the man.

PYRAMUS.
O wherefore, Nature, didst thou lions frame,
Since lion vile hath here deflower'd my dear?
Which is—no, no—which was the fairest dame

That liv'd, that lov'd, that lik'd, that look'd with cheer.
      Come, tears, confound!
      Out, sword, and wound
    The pap of Pyramus;
      Ay, that left pap,
      Where heart doth hop:
    Thus die I, thus, thus, thus.
      Now am I dead,
      Now am I fled;
    My soul is in the sky.
      Tongue, lose thy light!
      Moon, take thy flight!
    Now die, die, die, die, die.

[Dies. Exit Moonshine.]

DEMETRIUS.
No die, but an ace, for him; for he is but one.

LYSANDER.
Less than an ace, man; for he is dead, he is nothing.

THESEUS.
With the help of a surgeon he might yet recover and prove an ass.

HIPPOLYTA.
How chance Moonshine is gone before Thisbe comes back and finds her lover?

THESEUS.
She will find him by starlight.

Enter Thisbe.

Here she comes, and her passion ends the play.

HIPPOLYTA.
Methinks she should not use a long one for such a Pyramus. I hope she will be brief.

DEMETRIUS.
A mote will turn the balance, which Pyramus, which Thisbe, is the better: he for a man, God warrant us; she for a woman, God bless us!

LYSANDER.
She hath spied him already with those sweet eyes.

DEMETRIUS.
And thus she means, *videlicet*—

THISBE.
    Asleep, my love?
    What, dead, my dove?
O Pyramus, arise,
    Speak, speak. Quite dumb?
    Dead, dead? A tomb
Must cover thy sweet eyes.
    These lily lips,
    This cherry nose,
These yellow cowslip cheeks,
    Are gone, are gone!
    Lovers, make moan;
His eyes were green as leeks.
    O Sisters Three,
    Come, come to me,
With hands as pale as milk;
    Lay them in gore,
    Since you have shore
With shears his thread of silk.
    Tongue, not a word:
    Come, trusty sword,
Come, blade, my breast imbrue;
    And farewell, friends.
    Thus Thisbe ends.
Adieu, adieu, adieu.

[*Dies.*]

THESEUS.
Moonshine and Lion are left to bury the dead.

DEMETRIUS.
Ay, and Wall too.

BOTTOM.
No, I assure you; the wall is down that parted their fathers. Will it please you to see the epilogue, or to hear a Bergomask dance between two of our company?

77

THESEUS.
No epilogue, I pray you; for your play needs no excuse. Never excuse; for when the players are all dead there need none to be blamed. Marry, if he that writ it had played Pyramus, and hanged himself in Thisbe's garter, it would have been a fine tragedy; and so it is, truly; and very notably discharged. But come, your Bergomask; let your epilogue alone.

[*Here a dance of Clowns.*]

The iron tongue of midnight hath told twelve.
Lovers, to bed; 'tis almost fairy time.
I fear we shall outsleep the coming morn
As much as we this night have overwatch'd.
This palpable-gross play hath well beguil'd
The heavy gait of night. Sweet friends, to bed.
A fortnight hold we this solemnity
In nightly revels and new jollity.

[*Exeunt.*]

Enter Puck.

PUCK.
Now the hungry lion roars,
    And the wolf behowls the moon;
Whilst the heavy ploughman snores,
    All with weary task fordone.
Now the wasted brands do glow,
    Whilst the screech-owl, screeching loud,
Puts the wretch that lies in woe
    In remembrance of a shroud.
Now it is the time of night
    That the graves, all gaping wide,
Every one lets forth his sprite,
    In the church-way paths to glide.
And we fairies, that do run
    By the triple Hecate's team
From the presence of the sun,
    Following darkness like a dream,
Now are frolic; not a mouse
    Shall disturb this hallow'd house.
I am sent with broom before,
    To sweep the dust behind the door.

Enter Oberon and Titania with their Train.

OBERON.
  Through the house give glimmering light,
    By the dead and drowsy fire.
  Every elf and fairy sprite
    Hop as light as bird from brier,
  And this ditty after me,
  Sing and dance it trippingly.

TITANIA.
  First rehearse your song by rote,
    To each word a warbling note;
  Hand in hand, with fairy grace,
  Will we sing, and bless this place.

[*Song and Dance.*]

OBERON.
  Now, until the break of day,
  Through this house each fairy stray.
  To the best bride-bed will we,
  Which by us shall blessèd be;
  And the issue there create
  Ever shall be fortunate.
  So shall all the couples three
  Ever true in loving be;
  And the blots of Nature's hand
  Shall not in their issue stand:
  Never mole, hare-lip, nor scar,
  Nor mark prodigious, such as are
  Despised in nativity,
  Shall upon their children be.
  With this field-dew consecrate,
  Every fairy take his gait,
  And each several chamber bless,
  Through this palace, with sweet peace;
  And the owner of it blest.
  Ever shall it in safety rest,
  Trip away. Make no stay;
  Meet me all by break of day.

[*Exeunt Oberon, Titania and Train.*]

PUCK.

   If we shadows have offended,
   Think but this, and all is mended,
   That you have but slumber'd here
   While these visions did appear.
   And this weak and idle theme,
   No more yielding but a dream,
   Gentles, do not reprehend.
   If you pardon, we will mend.
   And, as I am an honest Puck,
   If we have unearnèd luck
   Now to 'scape the serpent's tongue,
   We will make amends ere long;
   Else the Puck a liar call.
   So, good night unto you all.
   Give me your hands, if we be friends,
   And Robin shall restore amends.

[Exit.]

THE SONNETS

I

From fairest creatures we desire increase,
That thereby beauty's rose might never die,
But as the riper should by time decease,
His tender heir might bear his memory:
But thou, contracted to thine own bright eyes,
Feed'st thy light's flame with self-substantial fuel,
Making a famine where abundance lies,
Thyself thy foe, to thy sweet self too cruel:
Thou that art now the world's fresh ornament,
And only herald to the gaudy spring,
Within thine own bud buriest thy content,
And tender churl mak'st waste in niggarding:
    Pity the world, or else this glutton be,
    To eat the world's due, by the grave and thee.

II

When forty winters shall besiege thy brow,
And dig deep trenches in thy beauty's field,
Thy youth's proud livery so gazed on now,
Will be a tatter'd weed of small worth held:
Then being asked, where all thy beauty lies,
Where all the treasure of thy lusty days;
To say, within thine own deep sunken eyes,
Were an all-eating shame, and thriftless praise.
How much more praise deserv'd thy beauty's use,
If thou couldst answer 'This fair child of mine
Shall sum my count, and make my old excuse,'
Proving his beauty by succession thine!
    This were to be new made when thou art old,
    And see thy blood warm when thou feel'st it cold.

III

Look in thy glass and tell the face thou viewest
Now is the time that face should form another;
Whose fresh repair if now thou not renewest,
Thou dost beguile the world, unbless some mother.
For where is she so fair whose unear'd womb
Disdains the tillage of thy husbandry?
Or who is he so fond will be the tomb,
Of his self-love to stop posterity?
Thou art thy mother's glass and she in thee
Calls back the lovely April of her prime;
So thou through windows of thine age shalt see,
Despite of wrinkles this thy golden time.
    But if thou live, remember'd not to be,
    Die single and thine image dies with thee.

IV

Unthrifty loveliness, why dost thou spend
Upon thy self thy beauty's legacy?
Nature's bequest gives nothing, but doth lend,
And being frank she lends to those are free:
Then, beauteous niggard, why dost thou abuse
The bounteous largess given thee to give?
Profitless usurer, why dost thou use
So great a sum of sums, yet canst not live?
For having traffic with thy self alone,
Thou of thy self thy sweet self dost deceive:
Then how when nature calls thee to be gone,
What acceptable audit canst thou leave?
    Thy unused beauty must be tombed with thee,
    Which, used, lives th' executor to be.

V

Those hours, that with gentle work did frame
The lovely gaze where every eye doth dwell,
Will play the tyrants to the very same
And that unfair which fairly doth excel;
For never-resting time leads summer on
To hideous winter, and confounds him there;
Sap checked with frost, and lusty leaves quite gone,

Beauty o'er-snowed and bareness every where:
Then were not summer's distillation left,
A liquid prisoner pent in walls of glass,
Beauty's effect with beauty were bereft,
Nor it, nor no remembrance what it was:
    But flowers distill'd, though they with winter meet,
    Leese but their show; their substance still lives sweet.

VI

Then let not winter's ragged hand deface,
In thee thy summer, ere thou be distill'd:
Make sweet some vial; treasure thou some place
With beauty's treasure ere it be self-kill'd.
That use is not forbidden usury,
Which happies those that pay the willing loan;
That's for thy self to breed another thee,
Or ten times happier, be it ten for one;
Ten times thy self were happier than thou art,
If ten of thine ten times refigur'd thee:
Then what could death do if thou shouldst depart,
Leaving thee living in posterity?
    Be not self-will'd, for thou art much too fair
    To be death's conquest and make worms thine heir.

VII

Lo! in the orient when the gracious light
Lifts up his burning head, each under eye
Doth homage to his new-appearing sight,
Serving with looks his sacred majesty;
And having climb'd the steep-up heavenly hill,
Resembling strong youth in his middle age,
Yet mortal looks adore his beauty still,
Attending on his golden pilgrimage:
But when from highmost pitch, with weary car,
Like feeble age, he reeleth from the day,
The eyes, 'fore duteous, now converted are
From his low tract, and look another way:
    So thou, thyself outgoing in thy noon:
    Unlook'd, on diest unless thou get a son.

VIII

Music to hear, why hear'st thou music sadly?
Sweets with sweets war not, joy delights in joy:
Why lov'st thou that which thou receiv'st not gladly,
Or else receiv'st with pleasure thine annoy?
If the true concord of well-tuned sounds,
By unions married, do offend thine ear,
They do but sweetly chide thee, who confounds
In singleness the parts that thou shouldst bear.
Mark how one string, sweet husband to another,
Strikes each in each by mutual ordering;
Resembling sire and child and happy mother,
Who, all in one, one pleasing note do sing:
    Whose speechless song being many, seeming one,
    Sings this to thee: 'Thou single wilt prove none.'

IX

Is it for fear to wet a widow's eye,
That thou consum'st thy self in single life?
Ah! if thou issueless shalt hap to die,
The world will wail thee like a makeless wife;
The world will be thy widow and still weep
That thou no form of thee hast left behind,
When every private widow well may keep
By children's eyes, her husband's shape in mind:
Look! what an unthrift in the world doth spend
Shifts but his place, for still the world enjoys it;
But beauty's waste hath in the world an end,
And kept unused the user so destroys it.
    No love toward others in that bosom sits
    That on himself such murd'rous shame commits.

X

For shame! deny that thou bear'st love to any,
Who for thy self art so unprovident.
Grant, if thou wilt, thou art belov'd of many,
But that thou none lov'st is most evident:
For thou art so possess'd with murderous hate,
That 'gainst thy self thou stick'st not to conspire,
Seeking that beauteous roof to ruinate

Which to repair should be thy chief desire.
O! change thy thought, that I may change my mind:
Shall hate be fairer lodg'd than gentle love?
Be, as thy presence is, gracious and kind,
Or to thyself at least kind-hearted prove:
    Make thee another self for love of me,
    That beauty still may live in thine or thee.

XI

As fast as thou shalt wane, so fast thou grow'st,
In one of thine, from that which thou departest;
And that fresh blood which youngly thou bestow'st,
Thou mayst call thine when thou from youth convertest,
Herein lives wisdom, beauty, and increase;
Without this folly, age, and cold decay:
If all were minded so, the times should cease
And threescore year would make the world away.
Let those whom nature hath not made for store,
Harsh, featureless, and rude, barrenly perish:
Look, whom she best endow'd, she gave thee more;
Which bounteous gift thou shouldst in bounty cherish:
    She carv'd thee for her seal, and meant thereby,
    Thou shouldst print more, not let that copy die.

XII

When I do count the clock that tells the time,
And see the brave day sunk in hideous night;
When I behold the violet past prime,
And sable curls, all silvered o'er with white;
When lofty trees I see barren of leaves,
Which erst from heat did canopy the herd,
And summer's green all girded up in sheaves,
Borne on the bier with white and bristly beard,
Then of thy beauty do I question make,
That thou among the wastes of time must go,
Since sweets and beauties do themselves forsake
And die as fast as they see others grow;
    And nothing 'gainst Time's scythe can make defence
    Save breed, to brave him when he takes thee hence.

XIII

O! that you were your self; but, love you are
No longer yours, than you your self here live:
Against this coming end you should prepare,
And your sweet semblance to some other give:
So should that beauty which you hold in lease
Find no determination; then you were
Yourself again, after yourself's decease,
When your sweet issue your sweet form should bear.
Who lets so fair a house fall to decay,
Which husbandry in honour might uphold,
Against the stormy gusts of winter's day
And barren rage of death's eternal cold?
    O! none but unthrifts. Dear my love, you know,
    You had a father: let your son say so.

XIV

Not from the stars do I my judgement pluck;
And yet methinks I have astronomy,
But not to tell of good or evil luck,
Of plagues, of dearths, or seasons' quality;
Nor can I fortune to brief minutes tell,
Pointing to each his thunder, rain and wind,
Or say with princes if it shall go well
By oft predict that I in heaven find:
But from thine eyes my knowledge I derive,
And constant stars in them I read such art
As 'Truth and beauty shall together thrive,
If from thyself, to store thou wouldst convert';
    Or else of thee this I prognosticate:
    'Thy end is truth's and beauty's doom and date.'

XV

When I consider every thing that grows
Holds in perfection but a little moment,
That this huge stage presenteth nought but shows
Whereon the stars in secret influence comment;
When I perceive that men as plants increase,
Cheered and checked even by the self-same sky,
Vaunt in their youthful sap, at height decrease,

And wear their brave state out of memory;
Then the conceit of this inconstant stay
Sets you most rich in youth before my sight,
Where wasteful Time debateth with decay
To change your day of youth to sullied night,
    And all in war with Time for love of you,
    As he takes from you, I engraft you new.

XVI

But wherefore do not you a mightier way
Make war upon this bloody tyrant, Time?
And fortify your self in your decay
With means more blessed than my barren rhyme?
Now stand you on the top of happy hours,
And many maiden gardens, yet unset,
With virtuous wish would bear you living flowers,
Much liker than your painted counterfeit:
So should the lines of life that life repair,
Which this, Time's pencil, or my pupil pen,
Neither in inward worth nor outward fair,
Can make you live your self in eyes of men.
    To give away yourself, keeps yourself still,
    And you must live, drawn by your own sweet skill.

XVII

Who will believe my verse in time to come,
If it were fill'd with your most high deserts?
Though yet heaven knows it is but as a tomb
Which hides your life, and shows not half your parts.
If I could write the beauty of your eyes,
And in fresh numbers number all your graces,
The age to come would say 'This poet lies;
Such heavenly touches ne'er touch'd earthly faces.'
So should my papers, yellow'd with their age,
Be scorn'd, like old men of less truth than tongue,
And your true rights be term'd a poet's rage
And stretched metre of an antique song:
    But were some child of yours alive that time,
    You should live twice,—in it, and in my rhyme.

XVIII

Shall I compare thee to a summer's day?
Thou art more lovely and more temperate:
Rough winds do shake the darling buds of May,
And summer's lease hath all too short a date:
Sometime too hot the eye of heaven shines,
And often is his gold complexion dimm'd,
And every fair from fair sometime declines,
By chance, or nature's changing course untrimm'd:
But thy eternal summer shall not fade,
Nor lose possession of that fair thou ow'st,
Nor shall death brag thou wander'st in his shade,
When in eternal lines to time thou grow'st,
    So long as men can breathe, or eyes can see,
    So long lives this, and this gives life to thee.

XIX

Devouring Time, blunt thou the lion's paws,
And make the earth devour her own sweet brood;
Pluck the keen teeth from the fierce tiger's jaws,
And burn the long-liv'd phoenix, in her blood;
Make glad and sorry seasons as thou fleets,
And do whate'er thou wilt, swift-footed Time,
To the wide world and all her fading sweets;
But I forbid thee one most heinous crime:
O! carve not with thy hours my love's fair brow,
Nor draw no lines there with thine antique pen;
Him in thy course untainted do allow
For beauty's pattern to succeeding men.
    Yet, do thy worst old Time: despite thy wrong,
    My love shall in my verse ever live young.

XX

A woman's face with nature's own hand painted,
Hast thou, the master mistress of my passion;
A woman's gentle heart, but not acquainted
With shifting change, as is false women's fashion:
An eye more bright than theirs, less false in rolling,
Gilding the object whereupon it gazeth;
A man in hue all 'hues' in his controlling,

Which steals men's eyes and women's souls amazeth.
And for a woman wert thou first created;
Till Nature, as she wrought thee, fell a-doting,
And by addition me of thee defeated,
By adding one thing to my purpose nothing.
    But since she prick'd thee out for women's pleasure,
    Mine be thy love and thy love's use their treasure.

XXI

So is it not with me as with that Muse,
Stirr'd by a painted beauty to his verse,
Who heaven itself for ornament doth use
And every fair with his fair doth rehearse,
Making a couplement of proud compare.
With sun and moon, with earth and sea's rich gems,
With April's first-born flowers, and all things rare,
That heaven's air in this huge rondure hems.
O! let me, true in love, but truly write,
And then believe me, my love is as fair
As any mother's child, though not so bright
As those gold candles fix'd in heaven's air:
    Let them say more that like of hearsay well;
    I will not praise that purpose not to sell.

XXII

My glass shall not persuade me I am old,
So long as youth and thou are of one date;
But when in thee time's furrows I behold,
Then look I death my days should expiate.
For all that beauty that doth cover thee,
Is but the seemly raiment of my heart,
Which in thy breast doth live, as thine in me:
How can I then be elder than thou art?
O! therefore love, be of thyself so wary
As I, not for myself, but for thee will;
Bearing thy heart, which I will keep so chary
As tender nurse her babe from faring ill.
    Presume not on thy heart when mine is slain,
    Thou gav'st me thine not to give back again.

XXIII

As an unperfect actor on the stage,
Who with his fear is put beside his part,
Or some fierce thing replete with too much rage,
Whose strength's abundance weakens his own heart;
So I, for fear of trust, forget to say
The perfect ceremony of love's rite,
And in mine own love's strength seem to decay,
O'ercharg'd with burthen of mine own love's might.
O! let my looks be then the eloquence
And dumb presagers of my speaking breast,
Who plead for love, and look for recompense,
More than that tongue that more hath more express'd.
   O! learn to read what silent love hath writ:
   To hear with eyes belongs to love's fine wit.

XXIV

Mine eye hath play'd the painter and hath stell'd,
Thy beauty's form in table of my heart;
My body is the frame wherein 'tis held,
And perspective it is best painter's art.
For through the painter must you see his skill,
To find where your true image pictur'd lies,
Which in my bosom's shop is hanging still,
That hath his windows glazed with thine eyes.
Now see what good turns eyes for eyes have done:
Mine eyes have drawn thy shape, and thine for me
Are windows to my breast, where-through the sun
Delights to peep, to gaze therein on thee;
   Yet eyes this cunning want to grace their art,
   They draw but what they see, know not the heart.

XXV

Let those who are in favour with their stars
Of public honour and proud titles boast,
Whilst I, whom fortune of such triumph bars
Unlook'd for joy in that I honour most.
Great princes' favourites their fair leaves spread
But as the marigold at the sun's eye,
And in themselves their pride lies buried,

For at a frown they in their glory die.
The painful warrior famoused for fight,
After a thousand victories once foil'd,
Is from the book of honour razed quite,
And all the rest forgot for which he toil'd:
    Then happy I, that love and am belov'd,
    Where I may not remove nor be remov'd.

XXVI

Lord of my love, to whom in vassalage
Thy merit hath my duty strongly knit,
To thee I send this written embassage,
To witness duty, not to show my wit:
Duty so great, which wit so poor as mine
May make seem bare, in wanting words to show it,
But that I hope some good conceit of thine
In thy soul's thought, all naked, will bestow it:
Till whatsoever star that guides my moving,
Points on me graciously with fair aspect,
And puts apparel on my tatter'd loving,
To show me worthy of thy sweet respect:
    Then may I dare to boast how I do love thee;
    Till then, not show my head where thou mayst prove me.

XXVII

Weary with toil, I haste me to my bed,
The dear respose for limbs with travel tir'd;
But then begins a journey in my head
To work my mind, when body's work's expired:
For then my thoughts—from far where I abide—
Intend a zealous pilgrimage to thee,
And keep my drooping eyelids open wide,
Looking on darkness which the blind do see:
Save that my soul's imaginary sight
Presents thy shadow to my sightless view,
Which, like a jewel hung in ghastly night,
Makes black night beauteous, and her old face new.
    Lo! thus, by day my limbs, by night my mind,
    For thee, and for myself, no quiet find.

XXVIII

How can I then return in happy plight,
That am debarre'd the benefit of rest?
When day's oppression is not eas'd by night,
But day by night and night by day oppress'd,
And each, though enemies to either's reign,
Do in consent shake hands to torture me,
The one by toil, the other to complain
How far I toil, still farther off from thee.
I tell the day, to please him thou art bright,
And dost him grace when clouds do blot the heaven:
So flatter I the swart-complexion'd night,
When sparkling stars twire not thou gild'st the even.
    But day doth daily draw my sorrows longer,
    And night doth nightly make grief's length seem stronger.

XXIX

When in disgrace with fortune and men's eyes
I all alone beweep my outcast state,
And trouble deaf heaven with my bootless cries,
And look upon myself, and curse my fate,
Wishing me like to one more rich in hope,
Featur'd like him, like him with friends possess'd,
Desiring this man's art, and that man's scope,
With what I most enjoy contented least;
Yet in these thoughts my self almost despising,
Haply I think on thee,— and then my state,
Like to the lark at break of day arising
From sullen earth, sings hymns at heaven's gate;
    For thy sweet love remember'd such wealth brings
    That then I scorn to change my state with kings.

XXX

When to the sessions of sweet silent thought
I summon up remembrance of things past,
I sigh the lack of many a thing I sought,
And with old woes new wail my dear time's waste:
Then can I drown an eye, unused to flow,
For precious friends hid in death's dateless night,
And weep afresh love's long since cancell'd woe,

And moan the expense of many a vanish'd sight:
Then can I grieve at grievances foregone,
And heavily from woe to woe tell o'er
The sad account of fore-bemoaned moan,
Which I new pay as if not paid before.
 But if the while I think on thee, dear friend,
 All losses are restor'd and sorrows end.

XXXI

Thy bosom is endeared with all hearts,
Which I by lacking have supposed dead;
And there reigns Love, and all Love's loving parts,
And all those friends which I thought buried.
How many a holy and obsequious tear
Hath dear religious love stol'n from mine eye,
As interest of the dead, which now appear
But things remov'd that hidden in thee lie!
Thou art the grave where buried love doth live,
Hung with the trophies of my lovers gone,
Who all their parts of me to thee did give,
That due of many now is thine alone:
 Their images I lov'd, I view in thee,
 And thou—all they—hast all the all of me.

XXXII

If thou survive my well-contented day,
When that churl Death my bones with dust shall cover
And shalt by fortune once more re-survey
These poor rude lines of thy deceased lover,
Compare them with the bett'ring of the time,
And though they be outstripp'd by every pen,
Reserve them for my love, not for their rhyme,
Exceeded by the height of happier men.
O! then vouchsafe me but this loving thought:
'Had my friend's Muse grown with this growing age,
A dearer birth than this his love had brought,
To march in ranks of better equipage:
 But since he died and poets better prove,
 Theirs for their style I'll read, his for his love'.

XXXIII

Full many a glorious morning have I seen
Flatter the mountain tops with sovereign eye,
Kissing with golden face the meadows green,
Gilding pale streams with heavenly alchemy;
Anon permit the basest clouds to ride
With ugly rack on his celestial face,
And from the forlorn world his visage hide,
Stealing unseen to west with this disgrace:
Even so my sun one early morn did shine,
With all triumphant splendour on my brow;
But out! alack! he was but one hour mine,
The region cloud hath mask'd him from me now.
    Yet him for this my love no whit disdaineth;
    Suns of the world may stain when heaven's sun staineth.

XXXIV

Why didst thou promise such a beauteous day,
And make me travel forth without my cloak,
To let base clouds o'ertake me in my way,
Hiding thy bravery in their rotten smoke?
'Tis not enough that through the cloud thou break,
To dry the rain on my storm-beaten face,
For no man well of such a salve can speak,
That heals the wound, and cures not the disgrace:
Nor can thy shame give physic to my grief;
Though thou repent, yet I have still the loss:
The offender's sorrow lends but weak relief
To him that bears the strong offence's cross.
    Ah! but those tears are pearl which thy love sheds,
    And they are rich and ransom all ill deeds.

XXXV

No more be griev'd at that which thou hast done:
Roses have thorns, and silver fountains mud:
Clouds and eclipses stain both moon and sun,
And loathsome canker lives in sweetest bud.
All men make faults, and even I in this,
Authorizing thy trespass with compare,
Myself corrupting, salving thy amiss,

94

Excusing thy sins more than thy sins are;
For to thy sensual fault I bring in sense,—
Thy adverse party is thy advocate,—
And 'gainst myself a lawful plea commence:
Such civil war is in my love and hate,
    That I an accessary needs must be,
    To that sweet thief which sourly robs from me.

XXXVI

Let me confess that we two must be twain,
Although our undivided loves are one:
So shall those blots that do with me remain,
Without thy help, by me be borne alone.
In our two loves there is but one respect,
Though in our lives a separable spite,
Which though it alter not love's sole effect,
Yet doth it steal sweet hours from love's delight.
I may not evermore acknowledge thee,
Lest my bewailed guilt should do thee shame,
Nor thou with public kindness honour me,
Unless thou take that honour from thy name:
    But do not so, I love thee in such sort,
    As thou being mine, mine is thy good report.

XXXVII

As a decrepit father takes delight
To see his active child do deeds of youth,
So I, made lame by Fortune's dearest spite,
Take all my comfort of thy worth and truth;
For whether beauty, birth, or wealth, or wit,
Or any of these all, or all, or more,
Entitled in thy parts, do crowned sit,
I make my love engrafted, to this store:
So then I am not lame, poor, nor despis'd,
Whilst that this shadow doth such substance give
That I in thy abundance am suffic'd,
And by a part of all thy glory live.
    Look what is best, that best I wish in thee:
    This wish I have; then ten times happy me!

XXXVIII

How can my muse want subject to invent,
While thou dost breathe, that pour'st into my verse
Thine own sweet argument, too excellent
For every vulgar paper to rehearse?
O! give thy self the thanks, if aught in me
Worthy perusal stand against thy sight;
For who's so dumb that cannot write to thee,
When thou thy self dost give invention light?
Be thou the tenth Muse, ten times more in worth
Than those old nine which rhymers invocate;
And he that calls on thee, let him bring forth
Eternal numbers to outlive long date.
    If my slight muse do please these curious days,
    The pain be mine, but thine shall be the praise.

XXXIX

O! how thy worth with manners may I sing,
When thou art all the better part of me?
What can mine own praise to mine own self bring?
And what is't but mine own when I praise thee?
Even for this, let us divided live,
And our dear love lose name of single one,
That by this separation I may give
That due to thee which thou deserv'st alone.
O absence! what a torment wouldst thou prove,
Were it not thy sour leisure gave sweet leave,
To entertain the time with thoughts of love,
Which time and thoughts so sweetly doth deceive,
    And that thou teachest how to make one twain,
    By praising him here who doth hence remain.

XL

Take all my loves, my love, yea take them all;
What hast thou then more than thou hadst before?
No love, my love, that thou mayst true love call;
All mine was thine, before thou hadst this more.
Then, if for my love, thou my love receivest,
I cannot blame thee, for my love thou usest;
But yet be blam'd, if thou thy self deceivest

By wilful taste of what thyself refusest.
I do forgive thy robbery, gentle thief,
Although thou steal thee all my poverty:
And yet, love knows it is a greater grief
To bear love's wrong, than hate's known injury.
 Lascivious grace, in whom all ill well shows,
 Kill me with spites yet we must not be foes.

XLI

Those pretty wrongs that liberty commits,
When I am sometime absent from thy heart,
Thy beauty, and thy years full well befits,
For still temptation follows where thou art.
Gentle thou art, and therefore to be won,
Beauteous thou art, therefore to be assail'd;
And when a woman woos, what woman's son
Will sourly leave her till he have prevail'd?
Ay me! but yet thou mightst my seat forbear,
And chide thy beauty and thy straying youth,
Who lead thee in their riot even there
Where thou art forced to break a twofold truth:—
 Hers by thy beauty tempting her to thee,
 Thine by thy beauty being false to me.

XLII

That thou hast her it is not all my grief,
And yet it may be said I loved her dearly;
That she hath thee is of my wailing chief,
A loss in love that touches me more nearly.
Loving offenders thus I will excuse ye:
Thou dost love her, because thou know'st I love her;
And for my sake even so doth she abuse me,
Suffering my friend for my sake to approve her.
If I lose thee, my loss is my love's gain,
And losing her, my friend hath found that loss;
Both find each other, and I lose both twain,
And both for my sake lay on me this cross:
 But here's the joy; my friend and I are one;
 Sweet flattery! then she loves but me alone.

XLIII

When most I wink, then do mine eyes best see,
For all the day they view things unrespected;
But when I sleep, in dreams they look on thee,
And darkly bright, are bright in dark directed.
Then thou, whose shadow shadows doth make bright,
How would thy shadow's form form happy show
To the clear day with thy much clearer light,
When to unseeing eyes thy shade shines so!
How would, I say, mine eyes be blessed made
By looking on thee in the living day,
When in dead night thy fair imperfect shade
Through heavy sleep on sightless eyes doth stay!
    All days are nights to see till I see thee,
    And nights bright days when dreams do show thee me.

XLIV

If the dull substance of my flesh were thought,
Injurious distance should not stop my way;
For then despite of space I would be brought,
From limits far remote, where thou dost stay.
No matter then although my foot did stand
Upon the farthest earth remov'd from thee;
For nimble thought can jump both sea and land,
As soon as think the place where he would be.
But, ah! thought kills me that I am not thought,
To leap large lengths of miles when thou art gone,
But that so much of earth and water wrought,
I must attend time's leisure with my moan;
    Receiving nought by elements so slow
    But heavy tears, badges of either's woe.

XLV

The other two, slight air, and purging fire
Are both with thee, wherever I abide;
The first my thought, the other my desire,
These present-absent with swift motion slide.
For when these quicker elements are gone
In tender embassy of love to thee,
My life, being made of four, with two alone

Sinks down to death, oppress'd with melancholy;
Until life's composition be recur'd
By those swift messengers return'd from thee,
Who even but now come back again, assur'd,
Of thy fair health, recounting it to me:
    This told, I joy; but then no longer glad,
    I send them back again, and straight grow sad.

XLVI

Mine eye and heart are at a mortal war,
How to divide the conquest of thy sight;
Mine eye my heart thy picture's sight would bar,
My heart mine eye the freedom of that right.
My heart doth plead that thou in him dost lie,—
A closet never pierc'd with crystal eyes—
But the defendant doth that plea deny,
And says in him thy fair appearance lies.
To side this title is impannelled
A quest of thoughts, all tenants to the heart;
And by their verdict is determined
The clear eye's moiety, and the dear heart's part:
    As thus; mine eye's due is thy outward part,
    And my heart's right, thy inward love of heart.

XLVII

Betwixt mine eye and heart a league is took,
And each doth good turns now unto the other:
When that mine eye is famish'd for a look,
Or heart in love with sighs himself doth smother,
With my love's picture then my eye doth feast,
And to the painted banquet bids my heart;
Another time mine eye is my heart's guest,
And in his thoughts of love doth share a part:
So, either by thy picture or my love,
Thyself away, art present still with me;
For thou not farther than my thoughts canst move,
And I am still with them, and they with thee;
    Or, if they sleep, thy picture in my sight
    Awakes my heart, to heart's and eye's delight.

XLVIII

How careful was I when I took my way,
Each trifle under truest bars to thrust,
That to my use it might unused stay
From hands of falsehood, in sure wards of trust!
But thou, to whom my jewels trifles are,
Most worthy comfort, now my greatest grief,
Thou best of dearest, and mine only care,
Art left the prey of every vulgar thief.
Thee have I not lock'd up in any chest,
Save where thou art not, though I feel thou art,
Within the gentle closure of my breast,
From whence at pleasure thou mayst come and part;
   And even thence thou wilt be stol'n I fear,
   For truth proves thievish for a prize so dear.

XLIX

Against that time, if ever that time come,
When I shall see thee frown on my defects,
When as thy love hath cast his utmost sum,
Call'd to that audit by advis'd respects;
Against that time when thou shalt strangely pass,
And scarcely greet me with that sun, thine eye,
When love, converted from the thing it was,
Shall reasons find of settled gravity;
Against that time do I ensconce me here,
Within the knowledge of mine own desert,
And this my hand, against my self uprear,
To guard the lawful reasons on thy part:
   To leave poor me thou hast the strength of laws,
   Since why to love I can allege no cause.

L

How heavy do I journey on the way,
When what I seek, my weary travel's end,
Doth teach that ease and that repose to say,
'Thus far the miles are measured from thy friend!'
The beast that bears me, tired with my woe,
Plods dully on, to bear that weight in me,
As if by some instinct the wretch did know

His rider lov'd not speed, being made from thee:
The bloody spur cannot provoke him on,
That sometimes anger thrusts into his hide,
Which heavily he answers with a groan,
More sharp to me than spurring to his side;
    For that same groan doth put this in my mind,
    My grief lies onward, and my joy behind.

LI

Thus can my love excuse the slow offence
Of my dull bearer when from thee I speed:
From where thou art why should I haste me thence?
Till I return, of posting is no need.
O! what excuse will my poor beast then find,
When swift extremity can seem but slow?
Then should I spur, though mounted on the wind,
In winged speed no motion shall I know,
Then can no horse with my desire keep pace;
Therefore desire, of perfect'st love being made,
Shall neigh—no dull flesh—in his fiery race;
But love, for love, thus shall excuse my jade,—
    'Since from thee going, he went wilful-slow,
    Towards thee I'll run, and give him leave to go.'

LII

So am I as the rich, whose blessed key,
Can bring him to his sweet up-locked treasure,
The which he will not every hour survey,
For blunting the fine point of seldom pleasure.
Therefore are feasts so solemn and so rare,
Since, seldom coming in that long year set,
Like stones of worth they thinly placed are,
Or captain jewels in the carcanet.
So is the time that keeps you as my chest,
Or as the wardrobe which the robe doth hide,
To make some special instant special-blest,
By new unfolding his imprison'd pride.
    Blessed are you whose worthiness gives scope,
    Being had, to triumph; being lacked, to hope.

LIII

What is your substance, whereof are you made,
That millions of strange shadows on you tend?
Since every one, hath every one, one shade,
And you but one, can every shadow lend.
Describe Adonis, and the counterfeit
Is poorly imitated after you;
On Helen's cheek all art of beauty set,
And you in Grecian tires are painted new:
Speak of the spring, and foison of the year,
The one doth shadow of your beauty show,
The other as your bounty doth appear;
And you in every blessed shape we know.
    In all external grace you have some part,
    But you like none, none you, for constant heart.

LIV

O! how much more doth beauty beauteous seem
By that sweet ornament which truth doth give.
The rose looks fair, but fairer we it deem
For that sweet odour, which doth in it live.
The canker blooms have full as deep a dye
As the perfumed tincture of the roses.
Hang on such thorns, and play as wantonly
When summer's breath their masked buds discloses:
But, for their virtue only is their show,
They live unwoo'd, and unrespected fade;
Die to themselves. Sweet roses do not so;
Of their sweet deaths, are sweetest odours made:
    And so of you, beauteous and lovely youth,
    When that shall vade, by verse distills your truth.

LV

Not marble, nor the gilded monuments
Of princes, shall outlive this powerful rhyme;
But you shall shine more bright in these contents
Than unswept stone, besmear'd with sluttish time.
When wasteful war shall statues overturn,
And broils root out the work of masonry,
Nor Mars his sword, nor war's quick fire shall burn

The living record of your memory.
'Gainst death, and all-oblivious enmity
Shall you pace forth; your praise shall still find room
Even in the eyes of all posterity
That wear this world out to the ending doom.
　　So, till the judgment that yourself arise,
　　You live in this, and dwell in lovers' eyes.

LVI

Sweet love, renew thy force; be it not said
Thy edge should blunter be than appetite,
Which but to-day by feeding is allay'd,
To-morrow sharpened in his former might:
So, love, be thou, although to-day thou fill
Thy hungry eyes, even till they wink with fulness,
To-morrow see again, and do not kill
The spirit of love, with a perpetual dulness.
Let this sad interim like the ocean be
Which parts the shore, where two contracted new
Come daily to the banks, that when they see
Return of love, more blest may be the view;
　　Or call it winter, which being full of care,
　　Makes summer's welcome, thrice more wished, more rare.

LVII

Being your slave what should I do but tend,
Upon the hours, and times of your desire?
I have no precious time at all to spend;
Nor services to do, till you require.
Nor dare I chide the world-without-end hour,
Whilst I, my sovereign, watch the clock for you,
Nor think the bitterness of absence sour,
When you have bid your servant once adieu;
Nor dare I question with my jealous thought
Where you may be, or your affairs suppose,
But, like a sad slave, stay and think of nought
Save, where you are, how happy you make those.
　　So true a fool is love, that in your will,
　　Though you do anything, he thinks no ill.

LVIII

That god forbid, that made me first your slave,
I should in thought control your times of pleasure,
Or at your hand the account of hours to crave,
Being your vassal, bound to stay your leisure!
O! let me suffer, being at your beck,
The imprison'd absence of your liberty;
And patience, tame to sufferance, bide each check,
Without accusing you of injury.
Be where you list, your charter is so strong
That you yourself may privilage your time
To what you will; to you it doth belong
Yourself to pardon of self-doing crime.
    I am to wait, though waiting so be hell,
    Not blame your pleasure be it ill or well.

LIX

If there be nothing new, but that which is
Hath been before, how are our brains beguil'd,
Which labouring for invention bear amiss
The second burthen of a former child!
O! that record could with a backward look,
Even of five hundred courses of the sun,
Show me your image in some antique book,
Since mind at first in character was done!
That I might see what the old world could say
To this composed wonder of your frame;
Wh'r we are mended, or wh'r better they,
Or whether revolution be the same.
    O! sure I am the wits of former days,
    To subjects worse have given admiring praise.

LX

Like as the waves make towards the pebbled shore,
So do our minutes hasten to their end;
Each changing place with that which goes before,
In sequent toil all forwards do contend.
Nativity, once in the main of light,
Crawls to maturity, wherewith being crown'd,
Crooked eclipses 'gainst his glory fight,

And Time that gave doth now his gift confound.
Time doth transfix the flourish set on youth
And delves the parallels in beauty's brow,
Feeds on the rarities of nature's truth,
And nothing stands but for his scythe to mow:
    And yet to times in hope, my verse shall stand.
    Praising thy worth, despite his cruel hand.

LXI

Is it thy will, thy image should keep open
My heavy eyelids to the weary night?
Dost thou desire my slumbers should be broken,
While shadows like to thee do mock my sight?
Is it thy spirit that thou send'st from thee
So far from home into my deeds to pry,
To find out shames and idle hours in me,
The scope and tenure of thy jealousy?
O, no! thy love, though much, is not so great:
It is my love that keeps mine eye awake:
Mine own true love that doth my rest defeat,
To play the watchman ever for thy sake:
    For thee watch I, whilst thou dost wake elsewhere,
    From me far off, with others all too near.

LXII

Sin of self-love possesseth all mine eye
And all my soul, and all my every part;
And for this sin there is no remedy,
It is so grounded inward in my heart.
Methinks no face so gracious is as mine,
No shape so true, no truth of such account;
And for myself mine own worth do define,
As I all other in all worths surmount.
But when my glass shows me myself indeed
Beated and chopp'd with tanned antiquity,
Mine own self-love quite contrary I read;
Self so self-loving were iniquity.
    'Tis thee,—myself,—that for myself I praise,
    Painting my age with beauty of thy days.

LXIII

Against my love shall be as I am now,
With Time's injurious hand crush'd and o'erworn;
When hours have drain'd his blood and fill'd his brow
With lines and wrinkles; when his youthful morn
Hath travell'd on to age's steepy night;
And all those beauties whereof now he's king
Are vanishing, or vanished out of sight,
Stealing away the treasure of his spring;
For such a time do I now fortify
Against confounding age's cruel knife,
That he shall never cut from memory
My sweet love's beauty, though my lover's life:
    His beauty shall in these black lines be seen,
    And they shall live, and he in them still green.

LXIV

When I have seen by Time's fell hand defac'd
The rich-proud cost of outworn buried age;
When sometime lofty towers I see down-raz'd,
And brass eternal slave to mortal rage;
When I have seen the hungry ocean gain
Advantage on the kingdom of the shore,
And the firm soil win of the watery main,
Increasing store with loss, and loss with store;
When I have seen such interchange of state,
Or state itself confounded, to decay;
Ruin hath taught me thus to ruminate—
That Time will come and take my love away.
    This thought is as a death which cannot choose
    But weep to have, that which it fears to lose.

LXV

Since brass, nor stone, nor earth, nor boundless sea,
But sad mortality o'ersways their power,
How with this rage shall beauty hold a plea,
Whose action is no stronger than a flower?
O! how shall summer's honey breath hold out,
Against the wrackful siege of battering days,
When rocks impregnable are not so stout,

106

Nor gates of steel so strong but Time decays?
O fearful meditation! where, alack,
Shall Time's best jewel from Time's chest lie hid?
Or what strong hand can hold his swift foot back?
Or who his spoil of beauty can forbid?
   O! none, unless this miracle have might,
   That in black ink my love may still shine bright.

LXVI

Tired with all these, for restful death I cry,
As to behold desert a beggar born,
And needy nothing trimm'd in jollity,
And purest faith unhappily forsworn,
And gilded honour shamefully misplac'd,
And maiden virtue rudely strumpeted,
And right perfection wrongfully disgrac'd,
And strength by limping sway disabled
And art made tongue-tied by authority,
And folly—doctor-like—controlling skill,
And simple truth miscall'd simplicity,
And captive good attending captain ill:
   Tir'd with all these, from these would I be gone,
   Save that, to die, I leave my love alone.

LXVII

Ah! wherefore with infection should he live,
And with his presence grace impiety,
That sin by him advantage should achieve,
And lace itself with his society?
Why should false painting imitate his cheek,
And steel dead seeming of his living hue?
Why should poor beauty indirectly seek
Roses of shadow, since his rose is true?
Why should he live, now Nature bankrupt is,
Beggar'd of blood to blush through lively veins?
For she hath no exchequer now but his,
And proud of many, lives upon his gains.
   O! him she stores, to show what wealth she had
   In days long since, before these last so bad.

LXVIII

Thus is his cheek the map of days outworn,
When beauty lived and died as flowers do now,
Before these bastard signs of fair were born,
Or durst inhabit on a living brow;
Before the golden tresses of the dead,
The right of sepulchres, were shorn away,
To live a second life on second head;
Ere beauty's dead fleece made another gay:
In him those holy antique hours are seen,
Without all ornament, itself and true,
Making no summer of another's green,
Robbing no old to dress his beauty new;
    And him as for a map doth Nature store,
    To show false Art what beauty was of yore.

LXIX

Those parts of thee that the world's eye doth view
Want nothing that the thought of hearts can mend;
All tongues—the voice of souls—give thee that due,
Uttering bare truth, even so as foes commend.
Thy outward thus with outward praise is crown'd;
But those same tongues, that give thee so thine own,
In other accents do this praise confound
By seeing farther than the eye hath shown.
They look into the beauty of thy mind,
And that in guess they measure by thy deeds;
Then—churls—their thoughts, although their eyes were kind,
To thy fair flower add the rank smell of weeds:
    But why thy odour matcheth not thy show,
    The soil is this, that thou dost common grow.

LXX

That thou art blam'd shall not be thy defect,
For slander's mark was ever yet the fair;
The ornament of beauty is suspect,
A crow that flies in heaven's sweetest air.
So thou be good, slander doth but approve
Thy worth the greater being woo'd of time;
For canker vice the sweetest buds doth love,

And thou present'st a pure unstained prime.
Thou hast passed by the ambush of young days
Either not assail'd, or victor being charg'd;
Yet this thy praise cannot be so thy praise,
To tie up envy, evermore enlarg'd,
    If some suspect of ill mask'd not thy show,
    Then thou alone kingdoms of hearts shouldst owe.

LXXI

No longer mourn for me when I am dead
Than you shall hear the surly sullen bell
Give warning to the world that I am fled
From this vile world with vilest worms to dwell:
Nay, if you read this line, remember not
The hand that writ it, for I love you so,
That I in your sweet thoughts would be forgot,
If thinking on me then should make you woe.
O! if,—I say you look upon this verse,
When I perhaps compounded am with clay,
Do not so much as my poor name rehearse;
But let your love even with my life decay;
    Lest the wise world should look into your moan,
    And mock you with me after I am gone.

LXXII

O! lest the world should task you to recite
What merit lived in me, that you should love
After my death,—dear love, forget me quite,
For you in me can nothing worthy prove;
Unless you would devise some virtuous lie,
To do more for me than mine own desert,
And hang more praise upon deceased I
Than niggard truth would willingly impart:
O! lest your true love may seem false in this
That you for love speak well of me untrue,
My name be buried where my body is,
And live no more to shame nor me nor you.
    For I am shamed by that which I bring forth,
    And so should you, to love things nothing worth.

LXXIII

That time of year thou mayst in me behold
When yellow leaves, or none, or few, do hang
Upon those boughs which shake against the cold,
Bare ruin'd choirs, where late the sweet birds sang.
In me thou see'st the twilight of such day
As after sunset fadeth in the west;
Which by and by black night doth take away,
Death's second self, that seals up all in rest.
In me thou see'st the glowing of such fire,
That on the ashes of his youth doth lie,
As the death-bed, whereon it must expire,
Consum'd with that which it was nourish'd by.
   This thou perceiv'st, which makes thy love more strong,
   To love that well, which thou must leave ere long.

LXXIV

But be contented: when that fell arrest
Without all bail shall carry me away,
My life hath in this line some interest,
Which for memorial still with thee shall stay.
When thou reviewest this, thou dost review
The very part was consecrate to thee:
The earth can have but earth, which is his due;
My spirit is thine, the better part of me:
So then thou hast but lost the dregs of life,
The prey of worms, my body being dead;
The coward conquest of a wretch's knife,
Too base of thee to be remembered.
   The worth of that is that which it contains,
   And that is this, and this with thee remains.

LXXV

So are you to my thoughts as food to life,
Or as sweet-season'd showers are to the ground;
And for the peace of you I hold such strife
As 'twixt a miser and his wealth is found.
Now proud as an enjoyer, and anon
Doubting the filching age will steal his treasure;
Now counting best to be with you alone,

Then better'd that the world may see my pleasure:
Sometime all full with feasting on your sight,
And by and by clean starved for a look;
Possessing or pursuing no delight,
Save what is had, or must from you be took.
    Thus do I pine and surfeit day by day,
    Or gluttoning on all, or all away.

LXXVI

Why is my verse so barren of new pride,
So far from variation or quick change?
Why with the time do I not glance aside
To new-found methods, and to compounds strange?
Why write I still all one, ever the same,
And keep invention in a noted weed,
That every word doth almost tell my name,
Showing their birth, and where they did proceed?
O! know sweet love I always write of you,
And you and love are still my argument;
So all my best is dressing old words new,
Spending again what is already spent:
    For as the sun is daily new and old,
    So is my love still telling what is told.

LXXVII

Thy glass will show thee how thy beauties wear,
Thy dial how thy precious minutes waste;
These vacant leaves thy mind's imprint will bear,
And of this book, this learning mayst thou taste.
The wrinkles which thy glass will truly show
Of mouthed graves will give thee memory;
Thou by thy dial's shady stealth mayst know
Time's thievish progress to eternity.
Look! what thy memory cannot contain,
Commit to these waste blanks, and thou shalt find
Those children nursed, deliver'd from thy brain,
To take a new acquaintance of thy mind.
    These offices, so oft as thou wilt look,
    Shall profit thee and much enrich thy book.

LXXVIII

So oft have I invoked thee for my Muse,
And found such fair assistance in my verse
As every alien pen hath got my use
And under thee their poesy disperse.
Thine eyes, that taught the dumb on high to sing
And heavy ignorance aloft to fly,
Have added feathers to the learned's wing
And given grace a double majesty.
Yet be most proud of that which I compile,
Whose influence is thine, and born of thee:
In others' works thou dost but mend the style,
And arts with thy sweet graces graced be;
    But thou art all my art, and dost advance
    As high as learning, my rude ignorance.

LXXIX

Whilst I alone did call upon thy aid,
My verse alone had all thy gentle grace;
But now my gracious numbers are decay'd,
And my sick Muse doth give an other place.
I grant, sweet love, thy lovely argument
Deserves the travail of a worthier pen;
Yet what of thee thy poet doth invent
He robs thee of, and pays it thee again.
He lends thee virtue, and he stole that word
From thy behaviour; beauty doth he give,
And found it in thy cheek: he can afford
No praise to thee, but what in thee doth live.
    Then thank him not for that which he doth say,
    Since what he owes thee, thou thyself dost pay.

LXXX

O! how I faint when I of you do write,
Knowing a better spirit doth use your name,
And in the praise thereof spends all his might,
To make me tongue-tied speaking of your fame!
But since your worth—wide as the ocean is,—
The humble as the proudest sail doth bear,
My saucy bark, inferior far to his,

On your broad main doth wilfully appear.
Your shallowest help will hold me up afloat,
Whilst he upon your soundless deep doth ride;
Or, being wrack'd, I am a worthless boat,
He of tall building, and of goodly pride:
    Then if he thrive and I be cast away,
    The worst was this,—my love was my decay.

LXXXI

Or I shall live your epitaph to make,
Or you survive when I in earth am rotten;
From hence your memory death cannot take,
Although in me each part will be forgotten.
Your name from hence immortal life shall have,
Though I, once gone, to all the world must die:
The earth can yield me but a common grave,
When you entombed in men's eyes shall lie.
Your monument shall be my gentle verse,
Which eyes not yet created shall o'er-read;
And tongues to be, your being shall rehearse,
When all the breathers of this world are dead;
    You still shall live,—such virtue hath my pen,—
    Where breath most breathes, even in the mouths of men.

LXXXII

I grant thou wert not married to my Muse,
And therefore mayst without attaint o'erlook
The dedicated words which writers use
Of their fair subject, blessing every book.
Thou art as fair in knowledge as in hue,
Finding thy worth a limit past my praise;
And therefore art enforced to seek anew
Some fresher stamp of the time-bettering days.
And do so, love; yet when they have devis'd,
What strained touches rhetoric can lend,
Thou truly fair, wert truly sympathiz'd
In true plain words, by thy true-telling friend;
    And their gross painting might be better us'd
    Where cheeks need blood; in thee it is abus'd.

LXXXIII

I never saw that you did painting need,
And therefore to your fair no painting set;
I found, or thought I found, you did exceed
That barren tender of a poet's debt:
And therefore have I slept in your report,
That you yourself, being extant, well might show
How far a modern quill doth come too short,
Speaking of worth, what worth in you doth grow.
This silence for my sin you did impute,
Which shall be most my glory being dumb;
For I impair not beauty being mute,
When others would give life, and bring a tomb.
    There lives more life in one of your fair eyes
    Than both your poets can in praise devise.

LXXXIV

Who is it that says most, which can say more,
Than this rich praise,—that you alone, are you?
In whose confine immured is the store
Which should example where your equal grew.
Lean penury within that pen doth dwell
That to his subject lends not some small glory;
But he that writes of you, if he can tell
That you are you, so dignifies his story,
Let him but copy what in you is writ,
Not making worse what nature made so clear,
And such a counterpart shall fame his wit,
Making his style admired every where.
    You to your beauteous blessings add a curse,
    Being fond on praise, which makes your praises worse.

LXXXV

My tongue-tied Muse in manners holds her still,
While comments of your praise richly compil'd,
Reserve their character with golden quill,
And precious phrase by all the Muses fil'd.
I think good thoughts, whilst others write good words,
And like unlettered clerk still cry 'Amen'
To every hymn that able spirit affords,

In polish'd form of well-refined pen.
Hearing you praised, I say "tis so, 'tis true,'
And to the most of praise add something more;
But that is in my thought, whose love to you,
Though words come hindmost, holds his rank before.
    Then others, for the breath of words respect,
    Me for my dumb thoughts, speaking in effect.

LXXXVI

Was it the proud full sail of his great verse,
Bound for the prize of all too precious you,
That did my ripe thoughts in my brain inhearse,
Making their tomb the womb wherein they grew?
Was it his spirit, by spirits taught to write,
Above a mortal pitch, that struck me dead?
No, neither he, nor his compeers by night
Giving him aid, my verse astonished.
He, nor that affable familiar ghost
Which nightly gulls him with intelligence,
As victors of my silence cannot boast;
I was not sick of any fear from thence:
    But when your countenance fill'd up his line,
    Then lacked I matter; that enfeebled mine.

LXXXVII

Farewell! thou art too dear for my possessing,
And like enough thou know'st thy estimate,
The charter of thy worth gives thee releasing;
My bonds in thee are all determinate.
For how do I hold thee but by thy granting?
And for that riches where is my deserving?
The cause of this fair gift in me is wanting,
And so my patent back again is swerving.
Thy self thou gav'st, thy own worth then not knowing,
Or me to whom thou gav'st it, else mistaking;
So thy great gift, upon misprision growing,
Comes home again, on better judgement making.
    Thus have I had thee, as a dream doth flatter,
    In sleep a king, but waking no such matter.

LXXXVIII

When thou shalt be dispos'd to set me light,
And place my merit in the eye of scorn,
Upon thy side, against myself I'll fight,
And prove thee virtuous, though thou art forsworn.
With mine own weakness, being best acquainted,
Upon thy part I can set down a story
Of faults conceal'd, wherein I am attainted;
That thou in losing me shalt win much glory:
And I by this will be a gainer too;
For bending all my loving thoughts on thee,
The injuries that to myself I do,
Doing thee vantage, double-vantage me.
    Such is my love, to thee I so belong,
    That for thy right, myself will bear all wrong.

LXXXIX

Say that thou didst forsake me for some fault,
And I will comment upon that offence:
Speak of my lameness, and I straight will halt,
Against thy reasons making no defence.
Thou canst not love disgrace me half so ill,
To set a form upon desired change,
As I'll myself disgrace; knowing thy will,
I will acquaintance strangle, and look strange;
Be absent from thy walks; and in my tongue
Thy sweet beloved name no more shall dwell,
Lest I, too much profane, should do it wrong,
And haply of our old acquaintance tell.
    For thee, against my self I'll vow debate,
    For I must ne'er love him whom thou dost hate.

XC

Then hate me when thou wilt; if ever, now;
Now, while the world is bent my deeds to cross,
Join with the spite of fortune, make me bow,
And do not drop in for an after-loss:
Ah! do not, when my heart hath 'scap'd this sorrow,
Come in the rearward of a conquer'd woe;
Give not a windy night a rainy morrow,

To linger out a purpos'd overthrow.
If thou wilt leave me, do not leave me last,
When other petty griefs have done their spite,
But in the onset come: so shall I taste
At first the very worst of fortune's might;
    And other strains of woe, which now seem woe,
    Compar'd with loss of thee, will not seem so.

XCI

Some glory in their birth, some in their skill,
Some in their wealth, some in their body's force,
Some in their garments though new-fangled ill;
Some in their hawks and hounds, some in their horse;
And every humour hath his adjunct pleasure,
Wherein it finds a joy above the rest:
But these particulars are not my measure,
All these I better in one general best.
Thy love is better than high birth to me,
Richer than wealth, prouder than garments' costs,
Of more delight than hawks and horses be;
And having thee, of all men's pride I boast:
    Wretched in this alone, that thou mayst take
    All this away, and me most wretchcd make.

XCII

But do thy worst to steal thyself away,
For term of life thou art assured mine;
And life no longer than thy love will stay,
For it depends upon that love of thine.
Then need I not to fear the worst of wrongs,
When in the least of them my life hath end.
I see a better state to me belongs
Than that which on thy humour doth depend:
Thou canst not vex me with inconstant mind,
Since that my life on thy revolt doth lie.
O! what a happy title do I find,
Happy to have thy love, happy to die!
    But what's so blessed-fair that fears no blot?
    Thou mayst be false, and yet I know it not.

XCIII

So shall I live, supposing thou art true,
Like a deceived husband; so love's face
May still seem love to me, though alter'd new;
Thy looks with me, thy heart in other place:
For there can live no hatred in thine eye,
Therefore in that I cannot know thy change.
In many's looks, the false heart's history
Is writ in moods, and frowns, and wrinkles strange.
But heaven in thy creation did decree
That in thy face sweet love should ever dwell;
Whate'er thy thoughts, or thy heart's workings be,
Thy looks should nothing thence, but sweetness tell.
    How like Eve's apple doth thy beauty grow,
    If thy sweet virtue answer not thy show!

XCIV

They that have power to hurt, and will do none,
That do not do the thing they most do show,
Who, moving others, are themselves as stone,
Unmoved, cold, and to temptation slow;
They rightly do inherit heaven's graces,
And husband nature's riches from expense;
They are the lords and owners of their faces,
Others, but stewards of their excellence.
The summer's flower is to the summer sweet,
Though to itself, it only live and die,
But if that flower with base infection meet,
The basest weed outbraves his dignity:
    For sweetest things turn sourest by their deeds;
    Lilies that fester, smell far worse than weeds.

XCV

How sweet and lovely dost thou make the shame
Which, like a canker in the fragrant rose,
Doth spot the beauty of thy budding name!
O! in what sweets dost thou thy sins enclose.
That tongue that tells the story of thy days,
Making lascivious comments on thy sport,
Cannot dispraise, but in a kind of praise;

Naming thy name, blesses an ill report.
O! what a mansion have those vices got
Which for their habitation chose out thee,
Where beauty's veil doth cover every blot
And all things turns to fair that eyes can see!
   Take heed, dear heart, of this large privilege;
   The hardest knife ill-us'd doth lose his edge.

XCVI

Some say thy fault is youth, some wantonness;
Some say thy grace is youth and gentle sport;
Both grace and faults are lov'd of more and less:
Thou mak'st faults graces that to thee resort.
As on the finger of a throned queen
The basest jewel will be well esteem'd,
So are those errors that in thee are seen
To truths translated, and for true things deem'd.
How many lambs might the stern wolf betray,
If like a lamb he could his looks translate!
How many gazers mightst thou lead away,
if thou wouldst use the strength of all thy state!
   But do not so; I love thee in such sort,
   As, thou being mine, mine is thy good report.

XCVII

How like a winter hath my absence been
From thee, the pleasure of the fleeting year!
What freezings have I felt, what dark days seen!
What old December's bareness everywhere!
And yet this time removed was summer's time;
The teeming autumn, big with rich increase,
Bearing the wanton burden of the prime,
Like widow'd wombs after their lords' decease:
Yet this abundant issue seem'd to me
But hope of orphans, and unfather'd fruit;
For summer and his pleasures wait on thee,
And, thou away, the very birds are mute:
   Or, if they sing, 'tis with so dull a cheer,
   That leaves look pale, dreading the winter's near.

XCVIII

From you have I been absent in the spring,
When proud-pied April, dress'd in all his trim,
Hath put a spirit of youth in every thing,
That heavy Saturn laugh'd and leap'd with him.
Yet nor the lays of birds, nor the sweet smell
Of different flowers in odour and in hue,
Could make me any summer's story tell,
Or from their proud lap pluck them where they grew:
Nor did I wonder at the lily's white,
Nor praise the deep vermilion in the rose;
They were but sweet, but figures of delight,
Drawn after you, you pattern of all those.
    Yet seem'd it winter still, and you away,
    As with your shadow I with these did play.

XCIX

The forward violet thus did I chide:
Sweet thief, whence didst thou steal thy sweet that smells,
If not from my love's breath? The purple pride
Which on thy soft cheek for complexion dwells
In my love's veins thou hast too grossly dy'd.
The lily I condemned for thy hand,
And buds of marjoram had stol'n thy hair;
The roses fearfully on thorns did stand,
One blushing shame, another white despair;
A third, nor red nor white, had stol'n of both,
And to his robbery had annex'd thy breath;
But, for his theft, in pride of all his growth
A vengeful canker eat him up to death.
    More flowers I noted, yet I none could see,
    But sweet, or colour it had stol'n from thee.

C

Where art thou Muse that thou forget'st so long,
To speak of that which gives thee all thy might?
Spend'st thou thy fury on some worthless song,
Darkening thy power to lend base subjects light?
Return forgetful Muse, and straight redeem,
In gentle numbers time so idly spent;

Sing to the ear that doth thy lays esteem
And gives thy pen both skill and argument.
Rise, resty Muse, my love's sweet face survey,
If Time have any wrinkle graven there;
If any, be a satire to decay,
And make time's spoils despised every where.
    Give my love fame faster than Time wastes life,
    So thou prevent'st his scythe and crooked knife.

CI

O truant Muse what shall be thy amends
For thy neglect of truth in beauty dy'd?
Both truth and beauty on my love depends;
So dost thou too, and therein dignified.
Make answer Muse: wilt thou not haply say,
'Truth needs no colour, with his colour fix'd;
Beauty no pencil, beauty's truth to lay;
But best is best, if never intermix'd'?
Because he needs no praise, wilt thou be dumb?
Excuse not silence so, for't lies in thee
To make him much outlive a gilded tomb
And to be prais'd of ages yet to be.
    Then do thy office, Muse; I teach thee how
    To make him seem long hence as he shows now.

CII

My love is strengthen'd, though more weak in seeming;
I love not less, though less the show appear;
That love is merchandiz'd, whose rich esteeming,
The owner's tongue doth publish every where.
Our love was new, and then but in the spring,
When I was wont to greet it with my lays;
As Philomel in summer's front doth sing,
And stops her pipe in growth of riper days:
Not that the summer is less pleasant now
Than when her mournful hymns did hush the night,
But that wild music burthens every bough,
And sweets grown common lose their dear delight.
    Therefore like her, I sometime hold my tongue:
    Because I would not dull you with my song.

121

CIII

Alack! what poverty my Muse brings forth,
That having such a scope to show her pride,
The argument, all bare, is of more worth
Than when it hath my added praise beside!
O! blame me not, if I no more can write!
Look in your glass, and there appears a face
That over-goes my blunt invention quite,
Dulling my lines, and doing me disgrace.
Were it not sinful then, striving to mend,
To mar the subject that before was well?
For to no other pass my verses tend
Than of your graces and your gifts to tell;
 And more, much more, than in my verse can sit,
 Your own glass shows you when you look in it.

CIV

To me, fair friend, you never can be old,
For as you were when first your eye I ey'd,
Such seems your beauty still. Three winters cold,
Have from the forests shook three summers' pride,
Three beauteous springs to yellow autumn turn'd,
In process of the seasons have I seen,
Three April perfumes in three hot Junes burn'd,
Since first I saw you fresh, which yet are green.
Ah! yet doth beauty like a dial-hand,
Steal from his figure, and no pace perceiv'd;
So your sweet hue, which methinks still doth stand,
Hath motion, and mine eye may be deceiv'd:
 For fear of which, hear this thou age unbred:
 Ere you were born was beauty's summer dead.

CV

Let not my love be call'd idolatry,
Nor my beloved as an idol show,
Since all alike my songs and praises be
To one, of one, still such, and ever so.
Kind is my love to-day, to-morrow kind,
Still constant in a wondrous excellence;
Therefore my verse to constancy confin'd,

One thing expressing, leaves out difference.
'Fair, kind, and true,' is all my argument,
'Fair, kind, and true,' varying to other words;
And in this change is my invention spent,
Three themes in one, which wondrous scope affords.
    Fair, kind, and true, have often liv'd alone,
    Which three till now, never kept seat in one.

CVI

When in the chronicle of wasted time
I see descriptions of the fairest wights,
And beauty making beautiful old rime,
In praise of ladies dead and lovely knights,
Then, in the blazon of sweet beauty's best,
Of hand, of foot, of lip, of eye, of brow,
I see their antique pen would have express'd
Even such a beauty as you master now.
So all their praises are but prophecies
Of this our time, all you prefiguring;
And for they looked but with divining eyes,
They had not skill enough your worth to sing:
    For we, which now behold these present days,
    Have eyes to wonder, but lack tongues to praise.

CVII

Not mine own fears, nor the prophetic soul
Of the wide world dreaming on things to come,
Can yet the lease of my true love control,
Supposed as forfeit to a confin'd doom.
The mortal moon hath her eclipse endur'd,
And the sad augurs mock their own presage;
Incertainties now crown themselves assur'd,
And peace proclaims olives of endless age.
Now with the drops of this most balmy time,
My love looks fresh, and Death to me subscribes,
Since, spite of him, I'll live in this poor rime,
While he insults o'er dull and speechless tribes:
    And thou in this shalt find thy monument,
    When tyrants' crests and tombs of brass are spent.

CVIII

What's in the brain, that ink may character,
Which hath not figur'd to thee my true spirit?
What's new to speak, what now to register,
That may express my love, or thy dear merit?
Nothing, sweet boy; but yet, like prayers divine,
I must each day say o'er the very same;
Counting no old thing old, thou mine, I thine,
Even as when first I hallow'd thy fair name.
So that eternal love in love's fresh case,
Weighs not the dust and injury of age,
Nor gives to necessary wrinkles place,
But makes antiquity for aye his page;
    Finding the first conceit of love there bred,
    Where time and outward form would show it dead.

CIX

O! never say that I was false of heart,
Though absence seem'd my flame to qualify,
As easy might I from my self depart
As from my soul which in thy breast doth lie:
That is my home of love: if I have rang'd,
Like him that travels, I return again;
Just to the time, not with the time exchang'd,
So that myself bring water for my stain.
Never believe though in my nature reign'd,
All frailties that besiege all kinds of blood,
That it could so preposterously be stain'd,
To leave for nothing all thy sum of good;
    For nothing this wide universe I call,
    Save thou, my rose, in it thou art my all.

CX

Alas! 'tis true, I have gone here and there,
And made my self a motley to the view,
Gor'd mine own thoughts, sold cheap what is most dear,
Made old offences of affections new;
Most true it is, that I have look'd on truth
Askance and strangely; but, by all above,
These blenches gave my heart another youth,

And worse essays prov'd thee my best of love.
Now all is done, save what shall have no end:
Mine appetite I never more will grind
On newer proof, to try an older friend,
A god in love, to whom I am confin'd.
    Then give me welcome, next my heaven the best,
    Even to thy pure and most most loving breast.

CXI

O! for my sake do you with Fortune chide,
The guilty goddess of my harmful deeds,
That did not better for my life provide
Than public means which public manners breeds.
Thence comes it that my name receives a brand,
And almost thence my nature is subdu'd
To what it works in, like the dyer's hand:
Pity me, then, and wish I were renew'd;
Whilst, like a willing patient, I will drink,
Potions of eisel 'gainst my strong infection;
No bitterness that I will bitter think,
Nor double penance, to correct correction.
    Pity me then, dear friend, and I assure ye,
    Even that your pity is enough to cure me.

CXII

Your love and pity doth the impression fill,
Which vulgar scandal stamp'd upon my brow;
For what care I who calls me well or ill,
So you o'er-green my bad, my good allow?
You are my all-the-world, and I must strive
To know my shames and praises from your tongue;
None else to me, nor I to none alive,
That my steel'd sense or changes right or wrong.
In so profound abysm I throw all care
Of others' voices, that my adder's sense
To critic and to flatterer stopped are.
Mark how with my neglect I do dispense:
    You are so strongly in my purpose bred,
    That all the world besides methinks are dead.

CXIII

Since I left you, mine eye is in my mind;
And that which governs me to go about
Doth part his function and is partly blind,
Seems seeing, but effectually is out;
For it no form delivers to the heart
Of bird, of flower, or shape which it doth latch:
Of his quick objects hath the mind no part,
Nor his own vision holds what it doth catch;
For if it see the rud'st or gentlest sight,
The most sweet favour or deformed'st creature,
The mountain or the sea, the day or night:
The crow, or dove, it shapes them to your feature.
    Incapable of more, replete with you,
    My most true mind thus maketh mine untrue.

CXIV

Or whether doth my mind, being crown'd with you,
Drink up the monarch's plague, this flattery?
Or whether shall I say, mine eye saith true,
And that your love taught it this alchemy,
To make of monsters and things indigest
Such cherubins as your sweet self resemble,
Creating every bad a perfect best,
As fast as objects to his beams assemble?
O! 'tis the first, 'tis flattery in my seeing,
And my great mind most kingly drinks it up:
Mine eye well knows what with his gust is 'greeing,
And to his palate doth prepare the cup:
    If it be poison'd, 'tis the lesser sin
    That mine eye loves it and doth first begin.

CXV

Those lines that I before have writ do lie,
Even those that said I could not love you dearer:
Yet then my judgment knew no reason why
My most full flame should afterwards burn clearer.
But reckoning Time, whose million'd accidents
Creep in 'twixt vows, and change decrees of kings,
Tan sacred beauty, blunt the sharp'st intents,

Divert strong minds to the course of altering things;
Alas! why fearing of Time's tyranny,
Might I not then say, 'Now I love you best,'
When I was certain o'er incertainty,
Crowning the present, doubting of the rest?
    Love is a babe, then might I not say so,
      To give full growth to that which still doth grow?

CXVI

Let me not to the marriage of true minds
Admit impediments. Love is not love
Which alters when it alteration finds,
Or bends with the remover to remove:
O, no! it is an ever-fixed mark,
That looks on tempests and is never shaken;
It is the star to every wandering bark,
Whose worth's unknown, although his height be taken.
Love's not Time's fool, though rosy lips and cheeks
Within his bending sickle's compass come;
Love alters not with his brief hours and weeks,
But bears it out even to the edge of doom.
    If this be error and upon me prov'd,
      I never writ, nor no man ever lov'd.

CXVII

Accuse me thus: that I have scanted all,
Wherein I should your great deserts repay,
Forgot upon your dearest love to call,
Whereto all bonds do tie me day by day;
That I have frequent been with unknown minds,
And given to time your own dear-purchas'd right;
That I have hoisted sail to all the winds
Which should transport me farthest from your sight.
Book both my wilfulness and errors down,
And on just proof surmise, accumulate;
Bring me within the level of your frown,
But shoot not at me in your waken'd hate;
    Since my appeal says I did strive to prove
      The constancy and virtue of your love.

CXVIII

Like as, to make our appetite more keen,
With eager compounds we our palate urge;
As, to prevent our maladies unseen,
We sicken to shun sickness when we purge;
Even so, being full of your ne'er-cloying sweetness,
To bitter sauces did I frame my feeding;
And, sick of welfare, found a kind of meetness
To be diseas'd, ere that there was true needing.
Thus policy in love, to anticipate
The ills that were not, grew to faults assur'd,
And brought to medicine a healthful state
Which, rank of goodness, would by ill be cur'd;
    But thence I learn and find the lesson true,
    Drugs poison him that so fell sick of you.

CXIX

What potions have I drunk of Siren tears,
Distill'd from limbecks foul as hell within,
Applying fears to hopes, and hopes to fears,
Still losing when I saw myself to win!
What wretched errors hath my heart committed,
Whilst it hath thought itself so blessed never!
How have mine eyes out of their spheres been fitted,
In the distraction of this madding fever!
O benefit of ill! now I find true
That better is, by evil still made better;
And ruin'd love, when it is built anew,
Grows fairer than at first, more strong, far greater.
    So I return rebuk'd to my content,
    And gain by ill thrice more than I have spent.

CXX

That you were once unkind befriends me now,
And for that sorrow, which I then did feel,
Needs must I under my transgression bow,
Unless my nerves were brass or hammer'd steel.
For if you were by my unkindness shaken,
As I by yours, you've pass'd a hell of time;
And I, a tyrant, have no leisure taken

To weigh how once I suffer'd in your crime.
O! that our night of woe might have remember'd
My deepest sense, how hard true sorrow hits,
And soon to you, as you to me, then tender'd
The humble salve, which wounded bosoms fits!
    But that your trespass now becomes a fee;
    Mine ransoms yours, and yours must ransom me.

CXXI

'Tis better to be vile than vile esteem'd,
When not to be receives reproach of being;
And the just pleasure lost, which is so deem'd
Not by our feeling, but by others' seeing:
For why should others' false adulterate eyes
Give salutation to my sportive blood?
Or on my frailties why are frailer spies,
Which in their wills count bad what I think good?
No, I am that I am, and they that level
At my abuses reckon up their own:
I may be straight though they themselves be bevel;
By their rank thoughts, my deeds must not be shown;
    Unless this general evil they maintain,
    All men are bad and in their badness reign.

CXXII

Thy gift, thy tables, are within my brain
Full character'd with lasting memory,
Which shall above that idle rank remain,
Beyond all date; even to eternity:
Or, at the least, so long as brain and heart
Have faculty by nature to subsist;
Till each to raz'd oblivion yield his part
Of thee, thy record never can be miss'd.
That poor retention could not so much hold,
Nor need I tallies thy dear love to score;
Therefore to give them from me was I bold,
To trust those tables that receive thee more:
    To keep an adjunct to remember thee
    Were to import forgetfulness in me.

CXXIII

No, Time, thou shalt not boast that I do change:
Thy pyramids built up with newer might
To me are nothing novel, nothing strange;
They are but dressings of a former sight.
Our dates are brief, and therefore we admire
What thou dost foist upon us that is old;
And rather make them born to our desire
Than think that we before have heard them told.
Thy registers and thee I both defy,
Not wondering at the present nor the past,
For thy records and what we see doth lie,
Made more or less by thy continual haste.
    This I do vow and this shall ever be;
    I will be true despite thy scythe and thee.

CXXIV

If my dear love were but the child of state,
It might for Fortune's bastard be unfather'd,
As subject to Time's love or to Time's hate,
Weeds among weeds, or flowers with flowers gather'd.
No, it was builded far from accident;
It suffers not in smiling pomp, nor falls
Under the blow of thralled discontent,
Whereto th' inviting time our fashion calls:
It fears not policy, that heretic,
Which works on leases of short-number'd hours,
But all alone stands hugely politic,
That it nor grows with heat, nor drowns with showers.
    To this I witness call the fools of time,
    Which die for goodness, who have lived for crime.

CXXV

Were't aught to me I bore the canopy,
With my extern the outward honouring,
Or laid great bases for eternity,
Which proves more short than waste or ruining?
Have I not seen dwellers on form and favour
Lose all and more by paying too much rent
For compound sweet; forgoing simple savour,

Pitiful thrivers, in their gazing spent?
No; let me be obsequious in thy heart,
And take thou my oblation, poor but free,
Which is not mix'd with seconds, knows no art,
But mutual render, only me for thee.
    Hence, thou suborned informer! a true soul
    When most impeach'd, stands least in thy control.

CXXVI

O thou, my lovely boy, who in thy power
Dost hold Time's fickle glass, his fickle hour;
Who hast by waning grown, and therein show'st
Thy lovers withering, as thy sweet self grow'st.
If Nature, sovereign mistress over wrack,
As thou goest onwards, still will pluck thee back,
She keeps thee to this purpose, that her skill
May time disgrace and wretched minutes kill.
Yet fear her, O thou minion of her pleasure!
She may detain, but not still keep, her treasure:
    Her audit (though delayed) answered must be,
    And her quietus is to render thee.

CXXVII

In the old age black was not counted fair,
Or if it were, it bore not beauty's name;
But now is black beauty's successive heir,
And beauty slander'd with a bastard shame:
For since each hand hath put on Nature's power,
Fairing the foul with Art's false borrowed face,
Sweet beauty hath no name, no holy bower,
But is profan'd, if not lives in disgrace.
Therefore my mistress' eyes are raven black,
Her eyes so suited, and they mourners seem
At such who, not born fair, no beauty lack,
Sland'ring creation with a false esteem:
    Yet so they mourn becoming of their woe,
    That every tongue says beauty should look so.

CXXVIII

How oft when thou, my music, music play'st,
Upon that blessed wood whose motion sounds

With thy sweet fingers when thou gently sway'st
The wiry concord that mine ear confounds,
Do I envy those jacks that nimble leap,
To kiss the tender inward of thy hand,
Whilst my poor lips which should that harvest reap,
At the wood's boldness by thee blushing stand!
To be so tickled, they would change their state
And situation with those dancing chips,
O'er whom thy fingers walk with gentle gait,
Making dead wood more bless'd than living lips.
    Since saucy jacks so happy are in this,
    Give them thy fingers, me thy lips to kiss.

CXXIX

The expense of spirit in a waste of shame
Is lust in action: and till action, lust
Is perjur'd, murderous, bloody, full of blame,
Savage, extreme, rude, cruel, not to trust;
Enjoy'd no sooner but despised straight;
Past reason hunted; and no sooner had,
Past reason hated, as a swallow'd bait,
On purpose laid to make the taker mad:
Mad in pursuit and in possession so;
Had, having, and in quest, to have extreme;
A bliss in proof,— and prov'd, a very woe;
Before, a joy propos'd; behind a dream.
    All this the world well knows; yet none knows well
    To shun the heaven that leads men to this hell.

CXXX

My mistress' eyes are nothing like the sun;
Coral is far more red, than her lips red:
If snow be white, why then her breasts are dun;
If hairs be wires, black wires grow on her head.
I have seen roses damask'd, red and white,
But no such roses see I in her cheeks;
And in some perfumes is there more delight
Than in the breath that from my mistress reeks.
I love to hear her speak, yet well I know
That music hath a far more pleasing sound:
I grant I never saw a goddess go,—
My mistress, when she walks, treads on the ground:

And yet by heaven, I think my love as rare,
As any she belied with false compare.

CXXXI

Thou art as tyrannous, so as thou art,
As those whose beauties proudly make them cruel;
For well thou know'st to my dear doting heart
Thou art the fairest and most precious jewel.
Yet, in good faith, some say that thee behold,
Thy face hath not the power to make love groan;
To say they err I dare not be so bold,
Although I swear it to myself alone.
And to be sure that is not false I swear,
A thousand groans, but thinking on thy face,
One on another's neck, do witness bear
Thy black is fairest in my judgment's place.
　　In nothing art thou black save in thy deeds,
　　And thence this slander, as I think, proceeds.

CXXXII

Thine eyes I love, and they, as pitying me,
Knowing thy heart torment me with disdain,
Have put on black and loving mourners be,
Looking with pretty ruth upon my pain.
And truly not the morning sun of heaven
Better becomes the grey cheeks of the east,
Nor that full star that ushers in the even,
Doth half that glory to the sober west,
As those two mourning eyes become thy face:
O! let it then as well beseem thy heart
To mourn for me since mourning doth thee grace,
And suit thy pity like in every part.
　　Then will I swear beauty herself is black,
　　And all they foul that thy complexion lack.

CXXXIII

Beshrew that heart that makes my heart to groan
For that deep wound it gives my friend and me!
Is't not enough to torture me alone,
But slave to slavery my sweet'st friend must be?

Me from myself thy cruel eye hath taken,
And my next self thou harder hast engross'd:
Of him, myself, and thee I am forsaken;
A torment thrice three-fold thus to be cross'd:
Prison my heart in thy steel bosom's ward,
But then my friend's heart let my poor heart bail;
Whoe'er keeps me, let my heart be his guard;
Thou canst not then use rigour in my jail:
    And yet thou wilt; for I, being pent in thee,
    Perforce am thine, and all that is in me.

CXXXIV

So, now I have confess'd that he is thine,
And I my self am mortgag'd to thy will,
Myself I'll forfeit, so that other mine
Thou wilt restore to be my comfort still:
But thou wilt not, nor he will not be free,
For thou art covetous, and he is kind;
He learn'd but surety-like to write for me,
Under that bond that him as fast doth bind.
The statute of thy beauty thou wilt take,
Thou usurer, that putt'st forth all to use,
And sue a friend came debtor for my sake;
So him I lose through my unkind abuse.
    Him have I lost; thou hast both him and me:
    He pays the whole, and yet am I not free.

CXXXV

Whoever hath her wish, thou hast thy 'Will,'
And 'Will' to boot, and 'Will' in over-plus;
More than enough am I that vex'd thee still,
To thy sweet will making addition thus.
Wilt thou, whose will is large and spacious,
Not once vouchsafe to hide my will in thine?
Shall will in others seem right gracious,
And in my will no fair acceptance shine?
The sea, all water, yet receives rain still,
And in abundance addeth to his store;
So thou, being rich in 'Will,' add to thy 'Will'
One will of mine, to make thy large will more.
    Let no unkind 'No' fair beseechers kill;
    Think all but one, and me in that one 'Will.'

CXXXVI

If thy soul check thee that I come so near,
Swear to thy blind soul that I was thy 'Will',
And will, thy soul knows, is admitted there;
Thus far for love, my love-suit, sweet, fulfil.
'Will', will fulfil the treasure of thy love,
Ay, fill it full with wills, and my will one.
In things of great receipt with ease we prove
Among a number one is reckon'd none:
Then in the number let me pass untold,
Though in thy store's account I one must be;
For nothing hold me, so it please thee hold
That nothing me, a something sweet to thee:
    Make but my name thy love, and love that still,
    And then thou lov'st me for my name is 'Will.'

CXXXVII

Thou blind fool, Love, what dost thou to mine eyes,
That they behold, and see not what they see?
They know what beauty is, see where it lies,
Yet what the best is take the worst to be.
If eyes, corrupt by over-partial looks,
Be anchor'd in the bay where all men ride,
Why of eyes' falsehood hast thou forged hooks,
Whereto the judgment of my heart is tied?
Why should my heart think that a several plot,
Which my heart knows the wide world's common place?
Or mine eyes, seeing this, say this is not,
To put fair truth upon so foul a face?
    In things right true my heart and eyes have err'd,
    And to this false plague are they now transferr'd.

CXXXVIII

When my love swears that she is made of truth,
I do believe her though I know she lies,
That she might think me some untutor'd youth,
Unlearned in the world's false subtleties.
Thus vainly thinking that she thinks me young,
Although she knows my days are past the best,
Simply I credit her false-speaking tongue:

On both sides thus is simple truth suppressed:
But wherefore says she not she is unjust?
And wherefore say not I that I am old?
O! love's best habit is in seeming trust,
And age in love, loves not to have years told:
    Therefore I lie with her, and she with me,
    And in our faults by lies we flatter'd be.

CXXXIX

O! call not me to justify the wrong
That thy unkindness lays upon my heart;
Wound me not with thine eye, but with thy tongue:
Use power with power, and slay me not by art,
Tell me thou lov'st elsewhere; but in my sight,
Dear heart, forbear to glance thine eye aside:
What need'st thou wound with cunning, when thy might
Is more than my o'erpress'd defence can bide?
Let me excuse thee: ah! my love well knows
Her pretty looks have been mine enemies;
And therefore from my face she turns my foes,
That they elsewhere might dart their injuries:
    Yet do not so; but since I am near slain,
    Kill me outright with looks, and rid my pain.

CXL

Be wise as thou art cruel; do not press
My tongue-tied patience with too much disdain;
Lest sorrow lend me words, and words express
The manner of my pity-wanting pain.
If I might teach thee wit, better it were,
Though not to love, yet, love to tell me so;—
As testy sick men, when their deaths be near,
No news but health from their physicians know;—
For, if I should despair, I should grow mad,
And in my madness might speak ill of thee;
Now this ill-wresting world is grown so bad,
Mad slanderers by mad ears believed be.
    That I may not be so, nor thou belied,
    Bear thine eyes straight, though thy proud heart go wide.

CXLI

In faith I do not love thee with mine eyes,
For they in thee a thousand errors note;
But 'tis my heart that loves what they despise,
Who, in despite of view, is pleased to dote.
Nor are mine ears with thy tongue's tune delighted;
Nor tender feeling, to base touches prone,
Nor taste, nor smell, desire to be invited
To any sensual feast with thee alone:
But my five wits nor my five senses can
Dissuade one foolish heart from serving thee,
Who leaves unsway'd the likeness of a man,
Thy proud heart's slave and vassal wretch to be:
    Only my plague thus far I count my gain,
    That she that makes me sin awards me pain.

CXLII

Love is my sin, and thy dear virtue hate,
Hate of my sin, grounded on sinful loving:
O! but with mine compare thou thine own state,
And thou shalt find it merits not reproving;
Or, if it do, not from those lips of thine,
That have profan'd their scarlet ornaments
And seal'd false bonds of love as oft as mine,
Robb'd others' beds' revenues of their rents.
Be it lawful I love thee, as thou lov'st those
Whom thine eyes woo as mine importune thee:
Root pity in thy heart, that, when it grows,
Thy pity may deserve to pitied be.
    If thou dost seek to have what thou dost hide,
    By self-example mayst thou be denied!

CXLIII

Lo, as a careful housewife runs to catch
One of her feather'd creatures broke away,
Sets down her babe, and makes all swift dispatch
In pursuit of the thing she would have stay;
Whilst her neglected child holds her in chase,
Cries to catch her whose busy care is bent
To follow that which flies before her face,

Not prizing her poor infant's discontent;
So runn'st thou after that which flies from thee,
Whilst I thy babe chase thee afar behind;
But if thou catch thy hope, turn back to me,
And play the mother's part, kiss me, be kind;
    So will I pray that thou mayst have thy 'Will,'
    If thou turn back and my loud crying still.

CXLIV

Two loves I have of comfort and despair,
Which like two spirits do suggest me still:
The better angel is a man right fair,
The worser spirit a woman colour'd ill.
To win me soon to hell, my female evil,
Tempteth my better angel from my side,
And would corrupt my saint to be a devil,
Wooing his purity with her foul pride.
And whether that my angel be turn'd fiend,
Suspect I may, yet not directly tell;
But being both from me, both to each friend,
I guess one angel in another's hell:
    Yet this shall I ne'er know, but live in doubt,
    Till my bad angel fire my good one out.

CXLV

Those lips that Love's own hand did make,
Breathed forth the sound that said 'I hate',
To me that languish'd for her sake:
But when she saw my woeful state,
Straight in her heart did mercy come,
Chiding that tongue that ever sweet
Was us'd in giving gentle doom;
And taught it thus anew to greet;
'I hate' she alter'd with an end,
That followed it as gentle day,
Doth follow night, who like a fiend
From heaven to hell is flown away.
    'I hate', from hate away she threw,
    And sav'd my life, saying 'not you'.

CXLVI

Poor soul, the centre of my sinful earth,
My sinful earth these rebel powers array,
Why dost thou pine within and suffer dearth,
Painting thy outward walls so costly gay?
Why so large cost, having so short a lease,
Dost thou upon thy fading mansion spend?
Shall worms, inheritors of this excess,
Eat up thy charge? Is this thy body's end?
Then soul, live thou upon thy servant's loss,
And let that pine to aggravate thy store;
Buy terms divine in selling hours of dross;
Within be fed, without be rich no more:
    So shall thou feed on Death, that feeds on men,
    And Death once dead, there's no more dying then.

CXLVII

My love is as a fever longing still,
For that which longer nurseth the disease;
Feeding on that which doth preserve the ill,
The uncertain sickly appetite to please.
My reason, the physician to my love,
Angry that his prescriptions are not kept,
Hath left me, and I desperate now approve
Desire is death, which physic did except.
Past cure I am, now Reason is past care,
And frantic-mad with evermore unrest;
My thoughts and my discourse as madmen's are,
At random from the truth vainly express'd;
    For I have sworn thee fair, and thought thee bright,
    Who art as black as hell, as dark as night.

CXLVIII

O me! what eyes hath Love put in my head,
Which have no correspondence with true sight;
Or, if they have, where is my judgment fled,
That censures falsely what they see aright?
If that be fair whereon my false eyes dote,
What means the world to say it is not so?
If it be not, then love doth well denote

Love's eye is not so true as all men's: no,
How can it? O! how can Love's eye be true,
That is so vexed with watching and with tears?
No marvel then, though I mistake my view;
The sun itself sees not, till heaven clears.
   O cunning Love! with tears thou keep'st me blind,
   Lest eyes well-seeing thy foul faults should find.

CXLIX

Canst thou, O cruel! say I love thee not,
When I against myself with thee partake?
Do I not think on thee, when I forgot
Am of my self, all tyrant, for thy sake?
Who hateth thee that I do call my friend,
On whom frown'st thou that I do fawn upon,
Nay, if thou lour'st on me, do I not spend
Revenge upon myself with present moan?
What merit do I in my self respect,
That is so proud thy service to despise,
When all my best doth worship thy defect,
Commanded by the motion of thine eyes?
   But, love, hate on, for now I know thy mind;
   Those that can see thou lov'st, and I am blind.

CL

O! from what power hast thou this powerful might,
With insufficiency my heart to sway?
To make me give the lie to my true sight,
And swear that brightness doth not grace the day?
Whence hast thou this becoming of things ill,
That in the very refuse of thy deeds
There is such strength and warrantise of skill,
That, in my mind, thy worst all best exceeds?
Who taught thee how to make me love thee more,
The more I hear and see just cause of hate?
O! though I love what others do abhor,
With others thou shouldst not abhor my state:
   If thy unworthiness rais'd love in me,
   More worthy I to be belov'd of thee.

CLI

Love is too young to know what conscience is,
Yet who knows not conscience is born of love?
Then, gentle cheater, urge not my amiss,
Lest guilty of my faults thy sweet self prove:
For, thou betraying me, I do betray
My nobler part to my gross body's treason;
My soul doth tell my body that he may
Triumph in love; flesh stays no farther reason,
But rising at thy name doth point out thee,
As his triumphant prize. Proud of this pride,
He is contented thy poor drudge to be,
To stand in thy affairs, fall by thy side.
    No want of conscience hold it that I call
    Her 'love,' for whose dear love I rise and fall.

CLII

In loving thee thou know'st I am forsworn,
But thou art twice forsworn, to me love swearing;
In act thy bed-vow broke, and new faith torn,
In vowing new hate after new love bearing:
But why of two oaths' breach do I accuse thee,
When I break twenty? I am perjur'd most;
For all my vows are oaths but to misuse thee,
And all my honest faith in thee is lost:
For I have sworn deep oaths of thy deep kindness,
Oaths of thy love, thy truth, thy constancy;
And, to enlighten thee, gave eyes to blindness,
Or made them swear against the thing they see;
    For I have sworn thee fair; more perjur'd I,
    To swear against the truth so foul a lie!

CLIII

Cupid laid by his brand and fell asleep:
A maid of Dian's this advantage found,
And his love-kindling fire did quickly steep
In a cold valley-fountain of that ground;
Which borrow'd from this holy fire of Love,
A dateless lively heat, still to endure,
And grew a seeting bath, which yet men prove

Against strange maladies a sovereign cure.
But at my mistress' eye Love's brand new-fired,
The boy for trial needs would touch my breast;
I, sick withal, the help of bath desired,
And thither hied, a sad distemper'd guest,
    But found no cure, the bath for my help lies
    Where Cupid got new fire; my mistress' eyes.

CLIV

The little Love-god lying once asleep,
Laid by his side his heart-inflaming brand,
Whilst many nymphs that vow'd chaste life to keep
Came tripping by; but in her maiden hand
The fairest votary took up that fire
Which many legions of true hearts had warm'd;
And so the general of hot desire
Was, sleeping, by a virgin hand disarm'd.
This brand she quenched in a cool well by,
Which from Love's fire took heat perpetual,
Growing a bath and healthful remedy,
For men diseas'd; but I, my mistress' thrall,
    Came there for cure and this by that I prove,
    Love's fire heats water, water cools not love.

www.ingramcontent.com/pod-product-compliance
Lightning Source LLC
Chambersburg PA
CBHW020139180626
46810CB00004B/1637